THE SKETCH

THE SKETCH
A GLEN ROCK MYSTERY

KAREN L. KIER

THE PAPER HOUSE
PUBLISHING

Copyright © 2024 by Karen L. Kier

All rights reserved.

Any references to historical events, real people, real events, or real places are used fictitiously. Names, characters, events, and places are products of the author's imagination.

No part of this book may be reproduced in any form or by any electronic or mechanical means, including information storage and retrieval systems, without written permission from the author, except for the use of brief quotations in a book review.

Second printing edition 2024

Forge Ahead Consulting 213 Wood Pond Loop Ponte Vedra, Fl, 32081

www.karenkier.com

CONTENTS

Chapter 1	1
Chapter 2	7
Chapter 3	13
Chapter 4	23
Chapter 5	35
Chapter 6	43
Chapter 7	53
Chapter 8	61
Chapter 9	71
Chapter 10	79
Chapter 11	87
Chapter 12	91
Chapter 13	99
Chapter 14	109
Chapter 15	115
Chapter 16	123
Chapter 17	129
Chapter 18	137
Chapter 19	145
Chapter 20	153
Chapter 21	161
Chapter 22	169
Chapter 23	179
Acknowledgments	185
About the Author	187

*Dedicated to my sons
Jeff, Joe, Ben, & Nick
Loving you, always!*

ONE

Dark clouds loomed out over the southeastern sky as Sally let her retriever out from the passenger side of her Chevy Blazer. "Okay, girl, we haven't got much time." She wondered if she'd make it out and back on her afternoon run before the predicted storms rolled in. She grabbed the leash off the seat in case it was needed, started the runner's app on her watch, and set off.

For late March, the afternoon was twenty degrees warmer than normal and it felt good to be out in shorts and a tee shirt. She made a mental note to watch for patches of melting ice between the stones and rotted leaves on the trail ahead. The air held deep musty scents of damp bark and moss and she breathed it in with relief.

After working in the heat of the bakery's sugary sweetness all day, she welcomed the contrast. Living over her bakery in the building she'd bought and renovated a few years ago made it easy for her to sneak out on late afternoons like this. Goldie, her faithful golden retriever, never disappointed with her own enthusiasm to run the local trails. Today, Sally was running later than she liked, but after her exhausting day, she was eager to zone out with a nice, easy-paced trek to help her destress.

Heading off on Eagle Trail, an eleven-mile loop that began behind the high school football field, she'd be sure to encounter a mix of flat, winding trails and a few pretty steep hills. The two bridges and numerous forks and rivulets that she'd pass would mark her progress as she went. The woods wrapped around the town, separating Glen Rock from the Upper Iowa River and was often frequented by hikers, mountain bikers, and runners like herself. Today however, she seemed to be the lone visitor.

She loved it like this, the times when she could shut down her brain from the day's noise, and just go. Chirps from the few birds that had stayed through winter and the ripple of a running stream made up the natural music she'd been wishing for all day. The cooling damp air as she approached the first twists in the trail braced her skin and her breath found a steady rhythm that matched her footfall. Goldie was familiar with the trail from years of running here and led the way at a good pace.

The quiet opened her mind to the day left behind. She'd read in the *Gazette* that morning that Charlie Webster, the grandfather of her old boyfriend, had passed away.

He was such a nice old man – so good to us when we were growing up, she reminisced.

Sally's thoughts of him led her back to the days when she was dating Finn. Sitting on the front porch swing, looking up at the stars, Finn had surprised her with their first kiss, taking them from childhood friends to forever sweethearts – or so she thought.

Finn, why didn't you come back to me? Where are you now? Are you coming for the funeral? Will you stay this time?

A tightness in her chest grew, reminding her she was still in love with him, even after all the years that had passed. She began wondering again what life would have been like if he'd stayed.

Would I even want to be with him now, after so much time apart? Yes, I would! Oh, why am I even thinking about this? The past is the past. Move on, girl.

Shaking the thoughts away, knowing that looking back at the past was fruitless, she calmed herself, taking in the beauty that surrounded her in the moment.

Deeper into the woods, not more than a few miles in, a sense of unease replaced the peace she'd been anticipating. The dark sky was closing in, threatening to end her run early.

We'll just go up the next hill and down to the bridge, and then head back, she thought.

Looking ahead, she saw Goldie stop short. Her tail was pointed straight back, and her hind quarters were set at a deep stance as the rest of her body began to shake. Sally caught up to her just as Goldie, staring ahead, bared her teeth and growled – a strange growl Sally had never heard before.

"What is it, girl?"

All at once, Goldie took off barking. Sally picked up her pace in pursuit. Cresting the hill and looking down at the culvert and bridge below, she saw the dog running towards three coyotes gnawing on their latest kill.

"Goldie - back!" she shouted as she caught up.

Two coyotes fled at the sight of her. Goldie stopped and stared down the lone predator that remained. He was bigger than the other two and towered over Goldie. Blood and saliva dangled from its chin.

Crouching, Sally grabbed the first three rocks she could find, then stood and began pummeling the dog's opponent. The third rock connected with the coyote's head and it turned away, yelping and running off into the woods.

Goldie didn't come when Sally called her again. Instead, the dog made her way to the culvert below where a stream flowed from under the bridge. Sally left the trail and climbed carefully down the steep bank, hoping her dog had no interest in the coyotes' prey.

As she got almost near enough to leash the retriever, she noticed a mud-splattered high-top sneaker, then blue jeans, and her eyes followed up the rest of the stretched-out remains.

Grabbing a branch nearby, she steadied herself. Vomit rose through her throat, and she turned to hurl. Shivering and shaken, she called to Goldie, who drew up to her side at the command. Sitting back on her heels, she wiped her chin with her shirt. Taking in as much air as she could, she let it out slowly. Then steadying herself, she knelt, one knee in the mud, and made a sign of the cross, silently asking for God's blessing on this person's soul. Then the fact hit her that this was the body of a young man.

Slowly, she regained strength in her legs and stood. Her mind raced. Who was this? In this small town, everyone knew everyone. She felt compelled to approach the body for a closer look.

Goldie, now leashed, stayed at her side as she stepped into the shallow stream. In another moment, she had to force herself to breathe through the revelation. She did know this boy.

The face, with skin now torn and blood smeared, was familiar though hardly recognizable. The brown curls that crowned the head and the green jacket he wore were unmistakable. Goldie knew him too, and sat down at the boy's feet, emitting soft whimpers.

He was just at work at the bakery yesterday. Oh, Jimmy, what's happened?

Thankful for cell service on her watch, Sally punched in the number for the local police.

"Glen Rock Police. What's your emergency?"

"This is Sally Andersen. Can I speak to the chief, please?" she asked, barely finding her voice.

"Bakery Sally?" the operator asked, in a cheerful tone. "It's Jeanie. What's wrong?"

"Jeanie, I found a body…out on Eagle Trail."

The woman's voice changed instantly. "Hold on. I'm putting you through to Tom now."

A brief minute passed. "Sally, what's going on?" the deep familiar voice asked.

"Tom, I'm up on Eagle Trail, about a mile in from the trailhead near the high school. There's a body here. He's dead, Tom."

"Okay, I'm on my way. Just stay there and wait for me. Don't touch anything."

"Tom, it's Jimmy Dalton."

There was a moment of silence before the chief could respond. "Jimmy…oh man."

"Hurry, please. Coyotes have already been here."

"That's how you found him?" Tom asked, bending over the body.

"Yup." Gruesome though it was, Sally had not been able to move more than a few feet away and leave the boy alone there in the cold running water. She hadn't taken her eyes off the scene.

Tom shook his head in disbelief of the site in front of him. Other uniformed officers and a medical team soon arrived with their equipment. Sally watched as the newcomers assessed the scene, whispering comments to each other.

"How does a seventeen-year-old high school senior, star quarterback, top of his class with a great future, end up dead in a culvert in the woods?" she asked, distressed by all she was witnessing.

"We'll find out, Sally. Why don't you head home, and I'll reach out in a day or so."

Back at the high school parking lot, as Goldie jumped into the Blazer, a bolt of lightning flashed around them, and the skies opened up, dropping rain like bullets.

TWO

Two days of pouring rain did nothing to wash away her memory of the dead boy's body she'd found. Preparing her famous apple pies in the back kitchen of the bakery, Sally tried to keep her mind from going to that dreadful scene. But each time she stepped into the attached café, it all came rushing back to her the minute her well-meaning patrons greeted her and offered up consoling thoughts. In addition to her loyal customers, others not so familiar seemed to show up and mix in with the crowd. Many lingered longer than usual, either to gossip or share a heroic story of the victim. Everyone seemed to know this boy and have an opinion of what happened to him.

While the police had been tight lipped with the media, the press wasted no time publishing Jimmy's picture on the front page of the *Gazette*. Sally had requested they keep her name out of the story, but they just couldn't resist, leaving her defenseless against her patrons' gossip and conversation.

Hey, I heard he took his own life.
I heard his girlfriend dumped him.
Kids these days...

It was Sally that found him, poor girl.
What were either of them doing out in those woods anyway?

Jen, who'd been working the counter, couldn't listen to anymore. Heading to the back kitchen for a break as soon as the crowd thinned out, she turned to Sally, who was busy putting a new batch of chocolate chip muffins in to bake.

"Can you believe this chatter? It's good for business but it's so sad. I just don't think I can take much more. Everyone's got a comment or an opinion."

"I know. It's hard," Sally consoled. "Most of those people knew him through his reputation playing football or his volunteering, or because of his parents. And many of those that didn't know him feel like they do because they've been reading about him in the local sports pages for the last four years. Maybe their talk isn't so much gossip as they just want to hold on to his memory. Maybe they feel closer to him here, knowing he worked for us."

"You might be right," Jen said as the bell over the front door rang.

"I'll get this customer. You take your break," Sally offered as she made her way to the front.

When Chief Tom Bashill walked in, there were dark circles under his eyes.

"Just a coffee today," Tom said, sliding two bills across the glass topped, oak bar. "Got a minute?" he asked, as Sally handed him his usual – a large dark roast.

"Sure. The morning rush is over. I'll get Jen to cover the counter." Filling her own coffee cup, Sally joined the police chief at a table along the wall away from the two mothers who lingered with their giggling children.

"How are you holding up?" she asked, stopping herself before adding that he looked terrible.

"Telling the family was the hardest. Debbie's visiting with

them today. She and some other women from the church are going over to help them plan the Mass and reception after. It'll be at the end of the week."

"We'll all be there," Sally said solemnly. She looked out the window beyond where they sat, noticing the rain splashing down. Her thoughts were interrupted by the bell that hung above the bakery door announcing the arrival of two men she'd never seen before, one wearing a Boston Red Sox cap. *That's unusual for these parts,* Sally thought to herself. Jen served them at the counter before they moved to sit at the table behind the chief.

"How are you doing, Sally?" Tom enquired. "I understand Jimmy worked here part time. This must be a hard time for you."

"I'm okay. Thanks for asking. Yes, he worked about ten hours a week for me. Mostly after school, weekends, school breaks. That sort of thing."

"What kind of work did he do for you?" Tom asked as he sat back and folded his arms.

"Well, his back still bothered him sometimes from that last tackle he took on the football field, so I kept it pretty light for him. Sweeping, general clean-up stuff. Once he got his license, I let him do a few deliveries for me. Truth is, he was good for the place. The patrons liked him. He was always so pleasant and polite. He got on good with my sister Nora, too. She hangs out here a lot with me now that she's aged out of school."

Tom nodded and continued his questioning. "His parents told me he used to like to help her with her artwork. Is that right?"

"Yup. He was a very talented artist. He did all the artwork on my menu boards. He liked Nora. She likes to sketch people she sees and paint pictures of Glen Rock. In fact, some of her landscape paintings are on these walls. Her work promotes the area and I promote her talent." Sally smiled as she gazed proudly across the room. "Anyway, they met at the community center where she goes sometimes. He volunteered there for extra school credit and he saw her working on a painting, so he gave her some tips and a lot of encouragement. She seemed to open up to him after that. He'd walk in the bakery and she'd beam, you know, all smiles. She doesn't do that for many people, not even around us sometimes. Why do you ask?"

"Just trying to get a better picture of the guy, that's all." Tom slowly took another sip of his coffee as if the act alone might help him sort his thoughts.

"Any progress in learning what happened to him?" Sally asked, half knowing that he couldn't really tell her anything since it was under investigation.

"Well, I can tell you this because the word is going to get out anyway." The chief leaned forward and lowered his voice. "The M.E.'s report showed that he didn't just suffer a fall. Sally, he had drugs in his system."

"What? No way. He was a good kid. What kind of drugs? The high school kids around here might chug a few beers at a party on Saturday nights, not that I condone that, but drugs really aren't their thing." Sally spoke like she was sure of it.

"The M.E. says he had Percocet laced with fentanyl in his system."

"Percocet! That's a painkiller. No way, I don't believe it. He didn't take drugs. It must have been a mistake. I know his back bothered him, but he got treatment. Did his parents tell you about that?" Sally asked.

"Yup. The doctor had given him a script for pain pills to help him with the physical therapy he needed, but he'd finished it. They thought he was fine and just taking some aspirin when it acted up."

"So how did he get Percocet?" Sally wanted to know.

"Not just Percocet," he reminded her. "Percocet laced with fentanyl."

"Well, where did that come from?" she persisted.

"Don't know. There's a lot of bad stuff out there. Maybe he bought it. Maybe someone slipped it to him. Maybe he thought it was aspirin. I don't know. We're still checking with people who know him, trying to figure out what he was doing that day and over the last weeks…that kind of stuff. We have his laptop and cellphone. We're checking it now to see if there's anything on it that will help us." The chief paused and then added, "I'm wondering if I can talk with Nora. Since they spent time together here and at the community center then maybe she saw something or knows something that can help."

"No way, Tom. You know she's autistic. She's already pretty torn up about this. When I told her about Jimmy, she lost it. She doesn't have a way of really telling us how she feels, so she either acts it out or sketches it out. My parents are keeping her home with them for a few days and Jen of course is always so eager to help, so she'll stop by to spend some time with her. We're trying to get Nora to draw what she feels but it's a long-shot right now." Sally felt bad she couldn't be more help to the chief. "Look, let's see how she is in a few days and I'll give you a call. She's going to the funeral with us and prayerfully, she'll find that healing."

"Ok, I get it Sally. No worries. When the time's right, but I can't wait too long." The chief swallowed the last of his coffee and looked around the bakery. The old farm tools that hung on the walls, intermingled with Nora's paintings, made it a warm and cozy place with appeal for both the young and the old. He felt relaxed for the first time since being called to the scene of Jimmy's death. "Hey, I heard Finn's grandfather passed away," he said, turning to Sally. "You going to the funeral tomorrow?"

Sally looked down into her coffee cup as if looking for the

answer. "I don't know. I should. He was a member of this community for a long time and of course, I always felt like I was part of their family, but I don't know. Lots of funerals all of a sudden. At least we know he died a quiet, peaceful death from being old. He lived a good life and saw a lot of changes in this town. I wonder what will happen to his old farm," Sally pondered aloud.

"Maybe Finn will come back," Tom suggested with a grin. Sally glanced at her friend, squeezed his hand, and gave him a half-smile before leaving to go back to work.

Once they were finished with their coffee, the two men rose from their seats behind where the chief still sat. Nikolai quietly made his way towards the kitchen, in search, he'd say if stopped, of the restrooms. Vic, pulling his cap down lower on his forehead, made his way around the bakery, lingering at the various paintings and artifacts that decorated the walls.

"Those are for sale," Sally offered, calling out from across the room.

The man nodded and when his partner returned from the back, they headed for their van parked across the street.

THREE

Looking out from the dirty, cracked kitchen window of his family's old farmhouse, Finn watched the storm rage against the fields while a new storm grew inside him. Coming back home after so long left him feeling unsettled. He hadn't been back since the day he'd buried his parents ten years before and staying at the old place was bringing back a lot of memories.

He could almost hear his father calling him from the barn and see his mother working in the garden. He was sure that staying in Des Moines after college had been the right decision but a small part of him wondered how his life would have been different if he'd come back to Glen Rock. He wondered how Sally was and what life with her would have been like.

Pushing those thoughts aside, he remembered his grandpa. He'd loved him and felt bad neglecting him in his last years. Now he'd just buried that wonderful, kind, humorous man.

Well, it's too late for regrets. No use looking back, he told himself.

Finn made his way to the diner in town for breakfast. From the booth where the waitress sat him, he could see the kitchen and his old friend Joe flipping pancakes in the back. The smell of brewing coffee warmed him. He turned to the young woman to place his order.

"I'll have a stack of pancakes, and could you ask the cook to put sugared cinnamon on them?"

The waitress made the note in her order book and snapped it shut before stuffing it into her apron pocket. "No problem, it might be a few minutes though. We've been swarmed with people all morning. Ever since they found that kid dead out by the high school, more people been coming in. They all want in on the latest news about it…like we know anything."

Ten minutes later, Joe, still in his white, grease-stained apron, approached Finn's table. "Hey, buddy! I guessed it was you by the order. You're the only one I know that eats pancakes that way and I heard your grampa's funeral was yesterday, so it fit. Sorry to hear he passed."

"Thanks, man." Finn reached out to shake hands, feeling Joe's firm grip. "How are you these days?"

"Great. Life is good. I now own the diner, and I have an apartment on the second floor above Sally's bakery. I'm keeping it simple. How 'bout you? What's it been, ten years?"

"Yup, just about. I'm living and working in Des Moines… financial planning and development. The insurance industry's big there." Finn gestured for Joe to join him.

"I can only sit for a minute. We're busy today," Joe said, taking the seat across. "Sounds like you're doing good. We've missed you, buddy."

"It's been a while for sure," Finn added remorsefully. "You know, after my parent's deaths, coming back just wasn't going to be the same."

"I get it. You were pretty broke up by their car accident. Drunk driver, right?"

"Yeah. Hey, what's this about Sally's bakery and a dead kid?" Finn asked, changing the subject.

"Sal's opened a great bakery. She renovated a three-story building further down on Main Street and lives on the top floor. How long you here for?"

"Heading back today."

"Well, check it out if you have time." Joe looked up to see a group of high school kids walk in. "Ah, kids. They're all creeped out since one of their friends was found dead on the trail behind the high school. Looks like drugs were involved. Sally's the one that found him. Listen, it's been great seeing you, but I gotta go back to work. Call me next visit and we'll hang out. There's lots of new stuff around town. A great place to take a vacation if you ever get to take one."

"Yeah, I will. Take care, Joe. Great seeing you."

Finn pushed aside his plate of half-eaten pancakes, paid his bill, and headed down the block to his lawyer's office on the corner of Court and Main Street. He noted the old tower clock at the center of town looked like it had been refurbished and a number of boutique stores and restaurants had replaced some of the old businesses.

It looks like this old town's coming back to life, he thought.

"Hey John," Finn said, seated across the desk from John Casey, the family's attorney. "How are you? Last we spoke, your wife was sick."

"Things are okay. She's getting chemo now. And the doctors have her on a lot of pills. I'll tell you, though, don't get old and don't get sick. It's so expensive. I might have to go and find myself a second job just to pay for all these doctors. But my girl's worth it. I'll do anything for her. Forty years we've been married."

"Wow, John. She's in my prayers. You both are."

"Thanks, Finn. Hey, your grandpa asked me to give you this letter. He knew when his last days were coming and figured you'd be back to collect his things. He loved you, Finn, and he trusted you. Now, I've been through the will and the old house and farm are yours. There's quite a little nest egg he's left you, too. I guess being the last living relative it all goes to you."

"John, I'm probably going to sell the farm. Can you handle it for me?"

"You sure you're not coming back?" John asked with appropriate concern.

"I doubt it," Finn said glumly.

"Hmmm…well, I might already have a lead on a buyer for you. Let me make some calls and I'll get back to you."

With business completed, Finn left the office, took one last look down Main Street, and got into his Jeep. About a mile down the road, heading out to Highway 52, Finn looked down and saw the letter from his grandpa sitting on the seat next to him. Curiosity, or maybe guilt at not spending more time with the old man, had him pulling off on a side road that had been taken over by weeds. He began to read.

"Dear Finn, I know you've come to bury me. If you're reading this, I've had my last breath. It's been a while since you've been back, but I knew you'd come. How's the house look? Run down? I guess we always thought you'd move back here. You could fix it up. I left enough money for that. I hope you think about it, but I know, you're probably going to sell.

Whatever you do with the money, be sure you use it for the good of others – don't just think about yourself. That's how you always know your decision's the right one. No matter what the problem, you won't go wrong with that golden rule.

THE SKETCH

You know, this town could use a smart guy like you. It's been through a lot of changes. Most of the farmers have moved on but some have stayed. There's still a lot of vacant properties but the last ten years have brought new life to some of the old businesses.

You got a girl yet? You know Sally's still here in town. She's got a great bakery. You should stop in and say "hello" and try one of those muffins she makes. They're better than your grandma's.

Hey, remember when you were young, we used to go fishing at Pine River Pond, out by the hotel? Best swimming hole for miles. We had so much fun. Remember the swing out behind the house and the picnics we used to have? Oh, your mother made the best chicken salad and lemonade. Too bad your own kids won't enjoy growing up here.

Well, I know, I'm rambling on, and you want to get back to your city life. I just wanted to take a minute to reminisce, and you know, say goodbye. Thanks for coming back to bury me. I do love you, Finn."

Finn rested his head on the steering wheel. He remembered climbing trees with Sally and throwing footballs with Tom at some of those picnics his grandfather mentioned. He remembered the time Sally's sister Nora found a bird with a broken wing and nursed it every day until it could fly away on its own. And he thought about the first time his father tried to teach him how to drive the tractor and about his mother getting him up to feed the chickens before school.

The letter stirred more memories of his childhood than he wanted to give thought to right now, and he felt a new ache in his chest. He noticed the morning clouds subsiding as he wiped the moist corners of his eyes. With a deep breath, he backed out of the dirt road, turned his Jeep around and headed back down Main Street to go try one of those muffins.

Inside the bakery, Sally was having another trying day. Customers continued to flood the bakery faster than she could keep up and she'd been left with little time for herself. She'd wanted to go to the funeral the day before for the grandfather of her old boyfriend but hadn't even been able to get away for that.

Her thoughts raced. *That old man was so giving and kind. He was so nice to me after Finn and I stopped dating. He made a point of stopping and asking how I was, like he knew my heart was broken and he just wanted to fix it for me.*

She remembered that Finn and his grandfather were really close, which is why she never understood why he'd stayed away so long. Now the old man was gone. Sally started to recall the times her family spent with Finn's, at each other's homes, at the park, at BBQs, and other town events. *It was like we were all one family. Finn was my best friend and my forever love, and now I wonder if I'll ever see him again.*

Sally started to think about how she and Finn had dated all through high school but parted as friends before heading off to college. It seemed the right thing to do at the time so they could both grow on their own. She'd tried to contact him a few times, but he refused her calls. She assumed he'd moved on without her. A few years later when his parents were killed in a car accident, she had reached out again. At their funeral, he had barely grumbled a "hello" to her, so she'd given him his space and stopped trying to connect.

OK, girl. Stop thinking about Finn and the past. You've got work to do, she told herself.

Sally pulled from the oven her famous sugar-topped blueberry muffins and headed out from the kitchen to the café side of the business to restock the counter. Just as the last muffin was placed, she looked up to see a Jeep pull into a space in front of the store. It didn't take long for her to figure out who it belonged to. She'd recognize those broad shoulders and that dark wavy hair anywhere. She felt her heart start to race and unconsciously, her hand went to the gold cross she was wearing – a gift Finn had given her for her last birthday when they were together as a couple.

Finn walked through the door and their eyes met. Sally felt the heat rise in her cheeks. Emotion threatened to overflow from her heart and give away the fact that she had never stopped loving him and always hoped he'd return and live his life with her forever. She held her breath and then slowly exhaled in effort to hide her feelings.

Finn gave a quick nod to Jen, who was wiping tables, and a wave to Nora, who had briefly looked up from her sketch pad. Nora's face lit up and she quietly began repeating in her own quiet voice, "Finn's back, Finn's back, Finn's back."

Finn made his way to the counter. "I'll have two muffins and two coffees," he said with his eyes now fixed again on Sally. He was surprised he felt so drawn to her, as if no time had passed at all since they were together back in the day.

"Finn, hi. How are you?" Sally asked stuffing her hands into her back pockets to hide the fact that they were shaking.

"I'm good. Can you join me? I just bought you a muffin and coffee hoping you could."

Sally laughed, releasing the tension she was holding, and came around the counter to greet him with a light friendly hug, hoping that was the appropriate thing to do after his long absence from her life. Finn surprised himself and her as he swept her up in his arms, unaware that everyone was watching their reunion. In that moment, emotion overwhelmed him, and he was sure this moment was somehow significant.

"It's so good to see you, Sally."

"Good to see you too, Finn," Sally said, taking in another deep breath to compose herself.

Jen noticed how flushed Sally's cheeks had become and

thought, *You've been praying he'd come back some day. I hope it works out for you, girlfriend.*

"I'll cover the counter," Jen said, waving her away. "Things have slowed down. You go. Take the afternoon if you want."

Sally followed Finn to a table in the corner after first turning to her friend to mouth the words, "Thank you."

"How's Nora doing?" Finn asked with concern.

"She's clearly happy to see you. She'll always remember how you stood up for her when the bullies came around. We'll both remember. You were good to her."

"Well, you were both like family. I'm just glad she's doing well."

"She's okay. She's still living with Mom and Dad and she's helping here part time. She still loves drawing and painting too. One of the high school kids that worked here was found dead and that's upset her, but I think she's doing better today."

"I heard you're the one that found him?"

"Yeah. Out on the trail. I was running with my dog, Goldie, and there he was. They know now he had drugs in his system, but no one knows where the drugs came from."

"That must have been difficult for you, finding him like that," Finn acknowledged, his concern evident by the intent expression on his face.

"It was awful seeing him stretched out in the cold water with no life left in his body. He was such a nice guy with a great future. Every day I hear about overdoses. It's usually in the big cities or other towns, but not here in Glen Rock. Tom's asking a lot of questions and I keep wondering if there's anything I can do to help him." She sat silent a minute, lost in thought, then added, "I sure would like to find out where Jimmy got those drugs. It had to be locally. We need to make sure this doesn't to happen anyone else."

Finn sat back in his chair marveling at how the woman in

front of him hadn't changed. She still had such a big heart and so much compassion for others. It was one of the things he had always loved about her. But her desire to find a potential drug dealer put a knot in his gut.

"Maybe you should just leave that to the police. You don't know who's selling these drugs. It could be dangerous," Finn cautioned.

Ignoring Finn's warning and changing the subject, she asked, "So how long are you in town?"

"I'm heading back now. I just came back for Grandpa's funeral."

"I'm sorry I couldn't get there. It just didn't work out with the bakery being so busy and all." Sally looked into his deep brown eyes, hoping he understood how badly she felt about missing it. Their eyes locked and undeniable emotion passed between them. Feeling the heat rise in her cheeks again, she turned away and asked, "What are you going to do with the farm?"

"I was thinking of selling it. I don't know. It won't do me much good living in Des Moines."

Sally couldn't ignore the twist she felt in her stomach at hearing his plan. *He's going to leave again,* she thought.

She sipped her coffee hoping to cover the sadness she suddenly felt. She knew she could never say anything to make him stay if he didn't really want to, so she decided to try to at least be supportive.

"I think the lot next to yours sold about six months ago. I don't know who bought it, but buyers seem to be in the area looking for properties. I haven't been out that way in a while. The town's been in transition over the last years, for the good, I think. There are some new shops that draw in tourists who come for the hiking, camping, and fishing. We've got some really cool farm-to-table restaurants now too. It's still the prettiest place on

Earth if you ask me. Maybe it's time to give us a try again. I mean, the town...a try again." Sally felt herself blushing again as she stumbled over her words.

"I agree," Finn said, gazing at Sally, thinking she was the prettiest woman on Earth.

Sally and Finn sat and continued to talk most of the afternoon until Sally finally got up from the table. "It's been great catching up Finn, but I have to go get Goldie. She's been waiting for me all day. Perhaps we can talk again? Maybe call once in a while?"

Finn looked at his watch and stood up. "Yeah, definitely. It's time I got on the road too." They parted giving each other a lingering hug. Finn left, grateful to his grandpa for the push, feeling more awake and alive than he'd felt in years. On his way out of town, back to Des Moines, he called his lawyer, John Casey.

"Hey John, it's Finn. Hold off on contacting that buyer you had for the farm. I want to think about it a little longer. I'm not sure yet, but I might just move back to town after all."

The lawyer couldn't delay the call he needed to make to his buyer with the bad news.

"Are you kidding me right now, Casey? First you think you have the farm to sell and then you don't. You said when the old guy croaked the kid wouldn't be back and it would be mine. You know I want that land to expand my business and I'm paying you handsomely to get it for me. Your wife's still sick and your debt's piling up, so do what I'm paying you to do."

Rodney slammed the phone into its cradle and sat back in his chair before pouring himself the glass of scotch that had been calling his name.

FOUR

Driving into Des Moines, Finn noticed that bright lights and tall buildings had replaced the beautiful countryside of Glen Rock. Finally, home after the three-hour drive, he struggled to sleep. The street noise bothered him for the first time he could remember. Agitated by something he couldn't name, he passed on his morning runs in the park. Opting instead to head straight for his corner office on the ninth floor, he kept himself busy with files, meetings, phone calls, and working late into the night. By mid-week, he couldn't hide the dark circles forming under his eyes.

"Hey, Finn. How're you doing? Everything ok? You look tired." His boss and close friend, Mike Billings, had taken a seat in one of the fine leather chairs across from Finn's desk.

"Yeah. Everything is good."

"All went well with the funeral?" Mike asked with concern.

Finn shrugged his shoulders and nodded. "Yeah. Fine."

"I see." Mike sat back and looked thoughtful. "Finn, you've been working round the clock since you're back. I don't think I've even seen you stop for lunch. When people do that, they're usually running toward something or from something. You already know your promotion's going to happen, so I know you're not trying to impress me. It must be something else. What's up?"

"Nothing gets under your radar, does it? Thanks for checking on me but everything's fine. I just have a lot of catching up to do after being away."

"I'm not sure I believe you," Mike said, leaning forward. "What happened back home? You know, you never say much about why you don't go back there." Mike smiled and continued to gently prod. "Is this about a girl?"

Finn gazed out over the city that swelled below his wall-to-wall window. "There isn't much to say. I was away at college when I got the call that my parents had been killed by a drunk driver. I'm still angry. That guy took so much from me that day. My old girlfriend, Sally, and I had already split up and without my folks, I never felt like I had a home to go back to after that. I just stayed here once I graduated, hoping to plant new roots."

"How's that working out for you?" Mike asked, his voice filled with compassion for his friend.

"Well, you're my family now, Mike. But I can't lie. Going back to Glen Rock woke something up inside me. I used to love that place. It's a beautiful small town, lots of country fresh air, and the nicest hard-working people. And yeah, I saw Sally. All week I've been thinking about what would have happened if I had moved back there instead of here all those years ago."

"Why did you and Sally break up?" Mike asked.

"We'd been best friends since childhood and dated all through high school. We didn't want our relationship to hold each other back once we got to college, so we agreed to separate and believed that if God meant for us to be together, we'd find our way back to each other in time."

"And you never went back after your parents died?" Mike asked in disbelief.

"No. I should have. My grandpa was there, and I wanted to see him, but it was just too hard to go back. I made excuses to avoid the memories."

"And Sally?" Mike probed.

"I've missed her. She was my best friend and I treated her horribly after we split up. She tried to call me a few times and I never returned her calls. I was afraid I'd go back on our promise to each other, to give each other a year. I loved her so much. I would have left college to be with her. And then when my parents died, I was just mean to everyone, including her. When I saw her this past week, she didn't even bring it up. That's the kind of girl she is, warm and loving."

Mike sat quiet for a moment and then added, "I want you to take the next week off. Take two if you need it. Go back home and take some time to figure everything out. It sounds like you're being pulled back there. If you're going to be taking that promotion we've discussed, when it comes through, you need to be all in here, in Des Moines. I'm saying that as your boss. As your friend, I think you need to go back and deal with things. If you don't, it will follow you around and haunt you forever."

Finn followed Mike's advice and headed back to Glen Rock the next day. Driving into town, the sight of Saint Benedict's Church, set back from the road and surrounded by its flower gardens, made his breath catch in his throat. Unable to take his eyes off the building, he pulled into the gravel lot and was pleased to find the doors unlocked when he approached.

Entering, he was struck by the sun streaming through the large stained-glass windows in the front. The church looked vibrant in contrast to how dark it felt the day of his grandpa's funeral. He knelt and said a prayer for his parents and grandpa and asked for guidance with the emotional struggle he knew he needed to face.

Sitting in silence his mind wandered. He began thinking about the person who had killed his parents.

The man had gotten drunk after losing his job that day. The police had said the guy had been both terrified and remorseful when he realized he'd caused the accident and that he cried and cried, even during the court proceedings. Please God, I know I've been away from the church for a while. I pushed away everything from my past with my parent's death. Please help me with this.

As he continued to pray, he could almost see the scene of the accident and feel the guy's pain. Wiping away a tear, he let out an audible sigh. He was ready to forgive the man and was sure his parents would want that too. The dull ache he'd been carrying began to fade, making way for a new sense of hope for his future.

Feeling renewed by an increased sense of peace and a clear head, Finn left the church and headed towards downtown. Stopping at the market, he picked up a few things he thought he might need for the weekend. Fully stocked with milk, cold cuts, and sandwich bread, he continued down Main Street, glancing over at the bakery as he passed. He felt a hint of regret at not calling Sally after their afternoon visit together.

Fifteen minutes later, as he drove over the stone bridge at the entrance of his family's property, he made a mental note that the mailbox was bent and would need repair. On the ground, smeared with years of dirt and debris, his mother's old farm stand sign lay abandoned. The arrow pointing up the drive and the words "FARM STORE: corn, cabbage, eggs, flowers, jams & jellies" were barely visible. Seeing the sign put a knot in his chest. Pushing away a longing for his parents, he drove on.

Willow trees with their overgrown hanging limbs lined the three-quarter-mile long driveway and he could see the old red barn and two other outbuildings in the distance.

Approaching the main house, he stopped and turned off his engine, taking a minute to take a good look at it. The window boxes his mother so lovingly filled each summer were soiled and stained from fallen autumn leaves and rusty rainwater that had dripped from wind-torn gutters. Roof shingles were missing, and an upstairs window was cracked. Next to it, though, the apple tree that had once hung the wooden swing his grandpa had put up for him, stood tall and proud, holding on to life and beckoning for more.

Walking into the old farmhouse, it struck him how much of his parents' heart and spirit were still there. He'd refused to see it during his last visit. But now the sunlight brought a warmth that he could almost breathe in.

Memories of growing up started flooding back and he felt the joy of his childhood again. Making room in the cupboards for his supplies, he thought of his mother and how she used to bustle about with so much energy. The kitchen was her command center for preserving her jellies and jams, drying leaves for tea, and arranging the flowers that she grew in the garden for later sale. Throwing open the window at the kitchen sink to get some air, he looked out at the barn and could almost hear his father calling to a younger Finn to come help fix the fencing in the back of the forty acres. It felt really good to be home.

―――

Nora was helping Sally in the bakery replacing coffee cups and covers next to the napkins and filling the sugar trays. She had her way of lining everything up in order. "Finn's back, Finn's back, Finn's back," she repeated in her hushed voice.

Sally was counting change at the register and heard her. "Nora, Finn's not back. He just stopped in last week for a coffee. I'm sorry, Nora, he couldn't stay."

"Finn's back, Finn's back, Finn's back. Jimmy's gone. Finn's back."

"Nora, honey, I know they've both been important to you and Jimmy is gone. But Finn's not back. He works in Des Moines, and you know that's far away from here. He was just here for a visit."

"Look." Nora pointed to her sketchbook sitting next to the register.

Sally looked at the last picture Nora had sketched. "That does look like him in his Jeep. Did you draw that the other day?"

"No, no, no. Now."

"You did this today? I wonder…. Hey Jen," Sally called over her shoulder. "Can you watch things for a while so I can go run an errand?"

"Sure. Take your time. Nora and I will be fine. Right, Nora?" she said putting her arm over Nora's shoulder.

Nora clapped her hands and smiled.

———

Finn was busy making a list of projects that needed to be done to fix up the old house when he heard a car making its way up the drive.

"Hello, is anyone here?" a familiar voice called out.

He recognized who it was right away. "Hey, Sally. How did you know I was here?"

Sally smiled up at him and handed him a brown box from The Bread Basket, her bakery.

"It's a small town, remember? Nora saw you drive past. She notices everything. I don't want to bother you, but I thought you might like some fresh donuts in the morning, if you're staying."

"Wow, thanks. Maple glazed. Mm mm. My favorite." He looked around the kitchen. "I'd offer you some coffee, but things are pretty dusty here. I haven't cleaned anything up."

"Would you like some help?" Sally offered. "You know, just to get the kitchen cleaned up a little so you're more comfortable? Jen's covering the bakery, so I have a little time."

"Sally, I can't ask you to do that. You'll get filthy."

"It won't bother me, Finn. That's what friends are for." Sally grabbed a towel from the counter.

"Look, Sally, I've been thinking, and I feel bad I haven't called you."

"That's okay, Finn. I know you were probably busy when you got back to work."

"Yes, I was. But what I mean is, I haven't called you for years. Not just that, but at my parents' funeral I was rude to you. We were friends and I treated you horribly. It's been bothering me how rotten I've been. Anyway, I'm sorry, Sally. I'm really sorry."

"It's okay, Finn. I understand. What happened to your parents, that was rough. You must have been going through a lot."

"Yeah, but I think it's time I got over it. I need to move passed the pain and anger. I've already missed so much because of it. I stopped at the church today on my way into town. It looked different, felt different too. I can't explain it, but it was like I had to stop there. It was so peaceful and beautiful. I'm ready to finally forgive the guy that hit my parents that night and make peace with what happened. It's been an eye-opener to have been back here. I think I actually miss the place a little."

"You might not miss it so much after you've been here a while," Sally remarked as her eyes scanned the room. "This place needs a lot of love."

Finn stood silent just looking at her, feeling blessed she was willing to forgive him. He knew a lot of women wouldn't do that. Sally was special, and he knew he better never forget that again.

"Here," Sally said, interrupting his thoughts, "let's grab that braided rug under the kitchen table and shake it out. There must be a broom around here somewhere to sweep the floor. Then we can see if the appliances still work. I don't know your plan, but you might need to get a dumpster if you're thinking of really fixing the place up."

Another car pulled up the drive and Finn looked out the window to see another one of his old friends. Heading out to greet him, he teased, "Well if it isn't the chief of police. How'd you know I was here?"

"I stopped by the bakery and Jen told me she suspected it's where I could find Sally. Hey, I thought you were rolling out of here right after the funeral. Didn't expect to see you so soon."

"I'm here for about a week or so. I needed some time to decide what I'm going to do with this old place."

"Sounds like a big decision. We'll have to catch up one night. Is Sally around?"

"Hey, Tom. What's up?" Sally asked, stepping out the front door to join them.

"I just wanted to give you an update and, well, to see if you've heard anything from the high school kids or anyone else who stops in the bakery. Has there been any talk about drugs or where Jimmy might have got them?"

"No, I can't think of anything. Mostly people just talk about what a good kid Jimmy was. The girls all miss him. Nothing unusual."

"We didn't find anything on his laptop or phone, or on his parents' computer. We're checking on the computers at the high school. Jimmy ever use your computer?"

Sally looked perplexed. "No. We have Wi-Fi there for the patrons. Anyone can use it. But, no, he never used my computer that I know of."

"If you think of anything, let me know. This fentanyl is becoming a problem. There was another overdose in Doylestown last night. Another kid. It's coming from somewhere."

"I'm guessing you talked to the boy's friends?" Sally asked.

"Yeah, but you know, they don't want to say anything to a cop. Besides, they all stick up for each other. No one wants to get in trouble."

"Well, maybe we can do some subtle asking around," Finn suggested.

Tom nodded. "As an alumni star athlete, maybe you could visit the coaches and check out the teams this week. Maybe something will come of it."

"That's a great idea." Sally's face lit up with the thought they might be helpful in finding out what happened to Jimmy. "I'll be a little more aggressive checking in with the kids when they come around the bakery and at the community center when I drop Nora off. We should get Joe on board too. I know the high school kids go into the diner all the time for burgers."

Tom shifted his weight to lean on the porch railing. "It's great you guys want to help but I don't know that you should get too involved."

Sally's eyes darted between the two men and determination swelled in her gut. "I found his body, Tom. I am involved."

"Okay, you're right. Let's plan to touch base in a couple days unless you find something substantial out in the meantime." He climbed back into his truck. Leaning his head out the window he added, "It's good to see you two together again."

Sally's cheeks reddened. Before she could correct him, he was already headed down the drive. Just as she and Finn were about to turn to go inside, another car approached. It was Sally's parents with Nora.

"Someone couldn't wait to see you, Finn," Mrs. Andersen said as she got out of the car followed by her husband. Nora exited the car holding on to a wrapped square package and made her way towards Finn.

"It's great to see you, Mr. and Mrs. Andersen. Hi, Nora! How did you all know I was here?"

"It's a small town," Sally reminded him as she winked.

"Nora's come with a gift and we're here to help with any clean-up if you want our help," Mr. Andersen offered. "Knowing the owners of the hardware store in town just might come in handy. Looks like the place needs a bit of work."

"Oh yeah!" Finn exclaimed looking back at the house. "All help is greatly accepted. But first, how's my friend Nora?" Finn approached Nora with open arms and waited to see if she would accept his offer for a hug. She stepped forward and handed him her gift. Finn sat on the front step and carefully unwrapped the package. His eyes grew wide when he uncovered a framed painting in oils of his family's home.

"Oh, Nora! It's beautiful. You did this for me? When? Wow! I don't know what to say."

Nora giggled, happy her gift had pleased him. "I knew, I knew, I knew. Finn's back. Finn's back." Nora jumped up and down and clapped her hands excitedly.

"She's been working on it for a while," Mrs. Andersen explained. "I think she started it when you left for college. She'd work on it and then put it away replacing it for another scene.

Then last week it came out again. She did it from a photograph taken a long time ago when you all hung out as kids."

"Nora, I love it. And I love you. You're the best." He stood and this time when he opened his arms to her, she accepted his hug.

FIVE

A few days later, Finn, Sally, and Joe huddled together at a corner table in the bakery waiting for Tom to join them. Late afternoons at the bakery were quiet and all the other tables were empty.

"A couple of the guys caved when I asked them about injuries on the team," Finn said. "It doesn't seem to matter if it's football, basketball, wrestling, or some other sport. They won't complain because if they do, the coaches won't let them play. If they don't play, they don't get scholarships."

"So, they try to manage their injuries by finding painkillers on their own?" Joe shook his head in disbelief.

"It sounds like it. And it's not like they have to go to some rough part of a neighboring town to get them. They said you can get anything you want online."

"How did you get all this information from them?" Sally asked.

"I plied them with pizza. It's what would have worked for me when I was their age." They were laughing at the thought of this when Tom walked in.

"It sounds like you started without me. I would have been here sooner but there was a break-in at the community center last night. Following up on it took my whole day."

"Finn will fill you in on what you missed. But how bad was the break-in?" Sally asked concerned.

"Nothing stolen. Mostly vandalism. The computers were smashed beyond use. Stuff was trashed around. They'll be closed a couple days cleaning up."

"That's terrible." Sally sighed. "I was just there yesterday. I donated some snacks for the after-school program, thinking it would give me a chance to talk to some of the kids who go there."

"What did you find out?" Tom asked.

"Not too much. I did ask some of the girls that stopped in the bakery how the basketball team was doing now that football season was over. They mentioned some of the guys had injuries they were playing through, but overall thought they were having a good season. I tried to ask about how they managed the injuries, and they didn't really want to say. I got the feeling there was something there, but they weren't sharing."

"I got a similar response from the kids at the diner," Joe added. "Any luck looking at the high school computers, Tom?"

"Nothing on the surface when we checked them. I'm guessing kids know that anything on those computers can be tracked and that teachers are probably checking them periodically. I wanted to check the computers at the community center, but they were vandalized and now that will be impossible. Thanks for trying, guys. I appreciate it. Let me know if you find out anything else."

Finn's phone rang and he excused himself from the table to take the call. While he was gone, Joe headed up to his apartment and Tom left to go back to the station. "This is so odd," he said to Sally as he sat back down. "That was John Casey. He says the buyer he has for my farm wants to increase his offer. John says he really wants the land. I tried to find out who the buyer was and what they wanted the land for, but John was tight-lipped. He said it was an outside firm from Boston and he couldn't say more."

"What are you going to do?"

"I told him I still don't know yet. I'm trying to figure some things out, like what I would do for work if I moved back. I don't want to farm the land, but I do wonder if I could do something different with it."

"Well, if you want to talk it through, you know where to find me." Sally looked around the bakery in case it wasn't obvious.

"Actually, I would. Would you like to go to dinner tonight?"

"Sure. Sounds great," she beamed.

Jen offered to open the bakery the next morning so Sally could sleep in an extra hour but, upon her arrival, she knew she'd have to get her up anyway.

Sally reached for her phone when it rang to see the caller ID. "Hi Jen, what's wrong?"

"Sally, sorry. I know you wanted to sleep in, but something's happened."

"What?"

"When I got here this morning, it looked like someone broke in last night."

"What? How? Are you okay?"

"Yeah, I'm okay. It looks like a brick was thrown through the window. It has a note stuck to it, held on by a rubber band. I haven't looked at it yet. I thought you might want to see it yourself or the police might want to see it as I found it. Sally, what should I do?"

"Stay where you are. I'll be right down." Sally quickly pulled on her jeans and tying her hair into a ponytail, charged downstairs.

After deliberating how serious the incident really was, Sally made a call to report it. It didn't take long before Tom arrived on the scene. Taking the note that had been wrapped around the brick, he laid it out on a table. The words, STOP OR ELSE, were written in large black letters.

"Looks like quite a mess here," Tom observed. "You don't have any security cameras, do you?"

"No, Tom." Sally folded her arms anticipating an argument. "I've always said cameras make people feel like they're being watched, and I refuse to think I can't trust the people who live and work in this town."

"In a situation like this, it might have told us who did this. I wish you'd rethink your decision. Times aren't what they used to be. Anyway, you can clean up the glass and repair the window if you want. I'll take the brick and note for now and keep it as evidence but situations like this don't go far. If it weren't for the note, I'd say it was a random act. But I think someone is clearly sending you a message."

Sally shrugged. "STOP OR ELSE. Stop what? Stop asking questions about Jimmy and drugs?"

"Maybe." Tom shook his head, looking apologetic. "I'm sorry you're involved in this."

"I'm not sorry if anything we find out can help."

"Now I'm wondering if the trouble at the community center was random," Tom said thinking aloud. "Listen, I know you'll want things cleaned up before you open for the day. If you think of anything else out of the ordinary or who might have it in for you, let me know. I'll head down to the diner now and see if Joe heard or saw anything suspicious before he left for work this morning. I'm sure he'd have called one of us if he did, but it's worth a try. I'll be in touch if I find out anything."

Sally and Jen worked to clean up the debris, and then Sally called her father to see if he could come fix the window.

"Of course, Sal," he responded, sounding concerned. "I'll be right over. I just can't understand who would do such a thing. I sure am glad you girls weren't there when it happened."

"Me too, Dad. And thanks." Sally hung up the phone and debated calling Finn. She decided he had enough on his plate, so she'd wait until later when she saw him in person.

Jen put some coffee to brew and began to prep the kitchen for the day's baking. "So, how was your date?"

"It was great. Like old times. We had a lot of fun."

"Think he'll move back?" Jen asked, eyeing her friend's reaction.

Sally smiled and reflected on her thoughts before answering. "I don't know. He likes it here but he's weighing his options about work. They're about to promote him and give him a big pay increase and he doesn't exactly have a job here. He's got a lot to think about."

Jen winked and flashed her friend a smile. "Well, he'd have you. What more could the man want?"

Finn stood barefoot in his kitchen waiting for his morning coffee to brew when he felt a draft. The trail of cool air led to the living room, where he tripped on the brick before noticing the broken window. He took a deep breath and sighed. His instinct was to call the police to report it, but he debated. *It must have happened last night while I was out or I would have heard the crash. Will it do any good if it was just some kids hanging out and letting off steam? We've never had trouble out here before. Of course, I haven't been here for ten years, so how would I know how things are? But was this really just random or does this have anything to do with the questions I asked the kids the other day? If that's the case, my determination to find out what happened to that boy has just doubled. No one's going to threaten me.*

It didn't take long for Tom to follow up by phone after Finn made the call to the station. "Your place has been vacant for a while, and I'm surprised there hasn't been more vandalism out there. But I'm not so sure this is random. You folks asked a lot of questions and I'm worried someone doesn't like it. First, the community center was vandalized and then Sally had a brick thrown through the window of her shop last night, and now you."

"She did? Is she okay?"

"Yes, she's fine. I just left her. Jen's with her now and her dad is on his way over to fix the broken window. I'll send someone out to your place to look at things. But listen, you folks need to be careful. I don't want you asking any more questions. And think about setting a light on a timer so it looks like you're there and maybe put up some cameras on the property."

"Thanks, Tom. I'll make a point to look into those things, and I'll check in with Sally later too. It's all a little unsettling. Clearly, times are changing."

———

Sitting in his car across the street, Vic reached for his cell phone. It rang a special chirp kept just for Rodney's calls. "Hey boss. It's done. Did it during the night. Some other girl found it and then the brunette came down and called the cops. She'll be too scared now to keep snoopin'. I'm sure of it. Dropped one at the boyfriend's house, too, while they were out. It was a good idea you had to place the bugs around town after that kid died. It gave us a chance to hear what's going on so we can make sure no trail leads back to us."

"If you hadn't gotten involved with locals, you wouldn't have this mess to clean up."

"Boss, we didn't know he was local. What happened to that kid aint' our fault."

"Find out where he ordered from and wipe any messages clean. And do whatever you got to do to keep them from asking more questions or we're going to have to shut them up."

"We're working on it." Vic heard a click, and knew the call was over.

SIX

Finn's time back in Glen Rock was almost over and he hadn't yet done everything he had hoped to do. He'd arranged with his boss to stay another week already and knew he couldn't extend his visit any longer. Utilizing the time he had, Finn devoted every minute to fixing up his family's old farmhouse. Taking breaks now and then from the manual labor, he offered to take Goldie for runs when Sally was working. Sometimes he'd just bring her out to the farm and let her run around. Goldie loved exploring the fields and Finn liked the companionship. He also liked Goldie's owner and knew if he had the dog, he'd probably also see Sally later in the day.

At week's end, he said his goodbyes and left. On the long drive back to Des Moines he reflected on his visit to Glen Rock and decided he felt happier than he'd been in many years. They hadn't gotten closer to finding out what happened to the boy that Sally found dead, but it had felt good to be involved in trying to solve the mystery. He'd also accomplished a lot of work on the house, and he knew he was falling more in love with Sally every day. His feelings for her had never gone away. *Am I actu-*

ally thinking of moving back? Time hasn't changed how I feel about Sally, but would she still want me after I've been gone for so long? Can I give up my job I worked so hard to get? Give up my promotion? And the money? Would I have to?

Returning to work, he was happy to be behind his desk. His muscles ached from all the manual work he had been doing over the last couple weeks. It was a good ache, but he needed the break. Mike showed up at his office door with an envelope in his hand and a huge grin.

"I'm here with good news. Your promotion's come through and I have all the paperwork right here." He waved the envelope in the air. "Congratulations, Finn. I'm so happy for you, buddy. You'll find all the details in here. As you know, the promotion comes with big money and even more benefits. And now, you're only one step away from becoming a full partner. Man, I can't think of anyone who deserves it more than you."

"Thanks. I'm not sure what to say. I guess I expected it to happen, but I thought it would probably be down the road a little bit." He shook Mike's hand and accepted the envelope.

"All you need to do is sign the paperwork."

"Okay, when do you need it back?"

"Well, I guess I'd expect you to sign it today. It's what you want, isn't it, Finn? It's what you've worked for. Are you having second thoughts?"

Finn hesitated. "Mike, I am so grateful for the promotion. I guess I got so busy in Glen Rock I haven't been thinking about my next steps here."

"Are you saying you have doubts? Finn, you better tell me what's going on." Mike closed the door and sat. Finn took the matching leather chair next to him.

"I don't know, Mike. Since I've been back home, it's like my world has changed. I really enjoyed my time there. I had fun for the first time in years…real fun. I reconnected with friends, did a lot of work on my family's home, and even got to help the chief of police with a case. And I'm in love with Sally. I always have been. She's been my best friend since we were little kids. But it's more than that too. I can't explain it. I love the town. It's a great place to raise kids." He quickly added, "It doesn't mean that I'm not still dedicated to my work here. I love my job. You know that. I'm wondering if there's any way I can have both."

Mike laughed. "Sounds like you're on the road to figuring out what you want. Maybe there is a way you can have most of it. Let's talk about options."

Finn arrived home that evening exhausted from the day's events and conversation about his job. After he pulled a frozen chicken dinner from the freezer and popped it in the microwave, he gave Sally a quick call. When it went to voicemail, he left her a message.

"Hey Sal, it's me, Finn. Give me a call when you get in later. I've got some ideas I want to share with you and see what you think. You know what, never mind. I'm going to try to clear my schedule and come out to Glen Rock later this week. I'll let you know my exact timetable, but please plan to meet up with me if you can get away from the bakery. How about a picnic lunch Friday at Pine River Pond? I'll bring the food."

Thursday night he left for Glen Rock with a new enthusiasm and anticipation for not only a great weekend ahead but for his whole future. By Friday morning, he had prepared everything needed for the perfect picnic lunch with Sally, and the weather was on his side. Sunny and seventy degrees were perfect for what he had planned.

When she arrived, he had already laid a plaid picnic blanket.

He held out a bouquet of wildflowers he'd picked from the field behind his house that morning, tied with a bright green bow.

"Oh, Finn, the flowers are so beautiful!"

"Just like you, Sal. Beautiful!"

"Thank you so much!" She turned her face up to his and kissed him. The lightness of her lips on his turned into deep passion as his arms wrapped around her slim waist. After several moments, Finn gently stepped back afraid of getting carried away in the moment.

With Goldie settled on a corner of the blanket, they sat down and enjoyed a lunch Finn had made of red grapes, provolone cheese, various meats, and Sicilian bread. Sally was anxious to hear the ideas Finn had mentioned in his phone message, but she didn't want to press him. Fortunately, he didn't make her wait too long.

"So, I've been giving my family's property a lot of thought, and what I should do with it," he began. "And I probably haven't mentioned this, but my grampa left me some money. I've used a little of it for the house renovations, but I'd like to do something with the rest that would really honor him, and then I've been thinking about the future. You know my promotion's come through."

"Finn, slow down. You're going in too many directions."

"Sorry, I'm just a little nervous. Excited, I mean. So, first things first because everything else hinges on one thing."

"Is this a riddle? What's the one thing?"

Finn got up from where he was sitting cross legged on the blanket and got down on bended knee, pulling out a ring box from his pocket. Opening it he asked, "Sally, will you and Goldie marry me?"

Hearing her name, Goldie jumped up, barked and put her front two paws on Finn's shoulders. "I take that as a yes from Goldie. What about you, Sally? I know I've been away a long time, and we haven't been back together all that long, but it all feels right. Will you marry me?"

Sally looked at the petite green emerald and diamond ring he held out to her. Her hands began shaking, and her eyes overflowed with tears. She didn't need to think long before replying. She had dreamed of this day her whole life. "Yes, yes, I'll marry you. Oh, Finn. I love you! I've always loved you. And the ring is beautiful."

"I love you too, Sally. I have loved you my whole life. I just can't imagine not having you in my life. I want to live with you, have kids with you, and grow old with you. The ring matches your eyes. It was my grandmother's so it's as special as you are."

Sally reached out and gave Finn a lingering kiss. They embraced until Goldie leapt on them, knocking them over to the ground. They laughed and gave Goldie belly rubs while she tried to lick their faces.

Catching their breaths, Finn recounted how the ring had been left for him after his grandfather had passed. "I think Gramps knew I'd be proposing to you one day and this was his way of saying he approved. Oh, and your father approved too!"

"Oh Finn, you asked him? That's so nice. I'm so excited to show my mom the ring. It's beautiful." She took a deep breath and added, "Now, I can't wait to hear the rest of your ideas. What are they?"

"Well," he began, "Assuming you're willing to live in our old farmhouse with me, I want to renovate the barn and property and make it into an event location. People could rent out the barn for weddings and other special events. And if we get started now, we could finish it by Christmas and our wedding reception could be the first one held there. That is if you're up for a Christmas wedding. I don't really want to wait even that long but, well, it will take time to get things together."

"A Christmas wedding! Yes, let's plan it. And I think the

barn redone could make a great event venue. There's tons of room for parking."

"I think there's enough room to have a brewery and small restaurant with just burgers, BBQ, and salads. I'm also thinking that we could set up a vendor's market for local farmers and craftspeople to sell some of their things. And we could have a small petting zoo so it would be a kid-friendly place to come.

"There's forty acres in total so with the right design we could really make it into something. And the barn and buildings are far enough away from the house I think that it'd really be separate from our residence. I'd have all local people do the work and then I want local people to work there when it's complete. One of the smaller side buildings close to the house will be kept for us for office space.

"Mike has agreed to let me try to work remotely. It means I won't get the promotion or the big raise but I'm okay with that. You could have some office space there for your bakery if you need it, and then we'll need someplace to manage the businesses on the property, like the bookings for the barn events and everything else going on. What do you think?"

"I think our kids will love it!" Sally said, bubbling over with happiness.

"And Sally, I want you to know, when the time comes, I'm willing to put an addition on the house for Nora. I haven't forgotten about her. I know she'll always need our support and I'm okay with that."

"Oh, Finn. Thank you." Sally reached out once again to embrace the man she had always loved.

Later that evening, out to dinner to celebrate their new future together, they noticed Tom and Debbie sitting at a table in the back of the restaurant. "Hi there," they said in unison as they approached their friends' table.

"We're here celebrating our anniversary," Debbie said. "How about you two?"

"We're celebrating our engagement!" Sally showed her new ring.

Joining them at their table reminded Finn of when they used to double-date in high school. Reminiscing about the old days and laughing with friends rekindled the feeling of home he had been missing. Moving back was indeed the right decision.

When Finn asked Tom about the progress in Jimmy's case, Tom became serious.

"There hasn't been any. We're at a dead end. It's so sad. There was another call on the scanner for EMS today. A ten-year-old boy was having a seizure from an overdose. It's gotten out of hand."

Sally became thoughtful. "That's terrible. I can't imagine being that kid's parent and not knowing how it happened or if it could have been prevented. It's all very troubling."

Later that night after Finn had dropped her back at her apartment, Sally started to think about what Tom had said about the drugs getting out of hand. *Drugs are becoming a real problem. How did Jimmy get his drugs? Who and where did it come from? There has to be an answer out there.*

Sally left her apartment on a hunch and went down to the bakery's kitchen where she did her office work. Turning on her computer she reviewed the search history and began scanning emails both received and sent. She reached for her cell phone and dialed Finn.

"You miss me already?" Finn chided.

"I've been thinking about what Tom said about that boy and the drugs. I started to question if Jimmy hadn't used my computer after all. I didn't think he knew my password or could get into it, and I never saw him using it, but I had to be sure, so I checked. I think I found something."

"What?"

"Going back through my history there are a bunch of searches to different sports doctors and sports pharmacies. In the trash folder there are some emails from different drug companies. They all have weird names that I never heard before. It looks like spam, but I can't be sure. It doesn't say much. It might just be sales. It could be nothing. I'm going to keep digging."

"It sounds like it might mean something but, it's late now. You should get some rest since you need to get up early. Tom said he was taking Debbie out of town for the weekend so it might have to wait until he's back anyway."

"You're right," she sighed.

"And Sal, don't tell anyone about this, okay? I don't want anyone threatening you again."

The next morning when Sally let Goldie back in from a quick trip to the yard to do her business, she noticed the dog hung her head low and laid down without eating. Her eyes were glassy. Sally wasted no time getting her to Doc Johnson, the local vet, who immediately ordered blood work and suggested Goldie spend the next 24 hours with him so he could give her IV fluids and monitor the situation.

Sally didn't like leaving Goldie but knew it was the right thing to do. There was definitely something wrong with the dog, but she was in good hands. Doc Johnson was another friend of theirs from school and she trusted him.

On the way back home, she phoned her mom and offered to have Nora sleep over at her apartment that night. She always cherished time with her sister and overnights gave her parent's a break. Having Nora visit would also distract her from worrying about Goldie.

That evening when Nora arrived, she made herself comfortable by the front window with her sketch pad in hand. Later she and Sally did a jigsaw puzzle together and then opted to watch a movie while dinner cooked. Later, they sat together on the couch looking through the stack of bridal magazines Sally had begun to collect. Once ready for bed, Nora sat at her favorite seat by the window and continued to draw. With the inside lights dimmed, she could see out, but no one could see her. She marveled at the brightness of the lights in the streets below. And for the second time that day, she drew a picture of the van and driver that sat across the street.

SEVEN

Finn welcomed a quiet evening at home after laying roofing shingles all day in the hot sun. As his shoulder muscles relaxed under the steamy hot water pulsating down from the shower head, his mind wandered to the future. He had so many ideas and was thrilled Sally seemed to be on board with them all. Still, a feeling of uncertainty overcame him when he thought of all that needed to be done before their Christmas wedding, and a brief wave of panic filled his gut when he wondered if he could pull it all together in time.

Knowing that Sally and Nora were having a girls' night together, he spent the remainder of his evening working up preliminary designs and specs for the barn and farm renovation. It was after midnight when he emailed them off to his architect friends in Des Moines, who would draw up what was needed for an initial presentation to the planning board for approval.

He fell right to sleep feeling satisfied with his accomplishments, but a few hours before daybreak, he woke hearing sirens. *It's not so different than being in the city,* he mused, rolling over and falling back to sleep. Waking again after what felt like only minutes, he looked at the clock next to the bed. Seeing the time, he jumped up and began to pull himself together. He had less than thirty minutes to spare before being late to pick Sally and Nora up for Sunday Mass.

Heading down Main Street, he saw red lights flashing and then noticed the smokey sky overhead. Pulling over to take in the scene, his pulse quickened and he felt every muscle in his body tighten. Bright orange flames leapt from the windows of Sally's building. The closer he drove, the more he was overwhelmed by oppressive heat and smoke. He instinctively said a silent prayer. *Please, God, let everyone be okay.*

Fire crews on the scene were hosing down flames that reignited as quickly as they were put out. An ambulance was parked across the street on standby. Finn noticed people milling around the sidewalk and assumed they'd been evacuated from neighboring buildings. He looked for anyone he knew but saw no one.

"Sally! Nora!" he called, jumping out of his Jeep and scanning the area. He had to find them. He rushed closer to where the ambulance parked and was confronted by Tom.

"Stay back, buddy," he shouted, as he grabbed Finn to pull him back. "You've got to let the fire crews do their work."

"What about Sally and her sister? And Joe?" Finn asked, breathless.

"The women got out. They're at the hospital. When the fire crews arrived, it was already bad."

"How bad? Sally and Nora, are they okay?" Finn pleaded.

"They're alive. That's all I can really tell you. It looked like they're pretty bad off. Sally was barely conscious, and Nora was out. The hospital's going to call me when they know more."

"Did you call their parents?" Finn asked, with urgency.

"Yes. They're heading over to the hospital. You could meet

them there. Look, before you go, there's more," Tom said cautiously.

"What more? Tell me."

"The fire chief called me on my cell phone as a courtesy. That's why I'm here and not still out of town with Debbie. It's Joe. He was home too. Finn, he didn't make it."

"Ugh! That poor guy." Finn shook his head in disbelief. "And his mother. Does she know?"

"We have someone going over to tell her now. We sent a medic with him just in case she takes it bad and needs any kind of treatment, you know, like a sedative or something."

"This is unbelievable. We just talked yesterday. We were all going to Mass this morning and then to brunch. I can't believe it. How did it happen?" Finn asked, still pleading for any information that would make sense of the situation.

"Too soon to tell. We'll check the appliances in the kitchen and the wiring, but everything was up to snuff when the building was remodeled. There'll be an investigation. I've got to get back to the fire chief now. You can hang tight here or head to the hospital. It might be good if you meet up with the Andersens though. They're going to need everyone's support. To be honest," he added, "Nora's in such bad shape, I'll be surprised if she makes it at all." Tom turned and left Finn standing there dazed.

Walking back to his Jeep, Finn took a last look at the scene. He pulled away from the curb and raced toward the hospital, silently praying for his best friend and her sister. Arriving at the hospital's emergency entrance, he found the Andersens sitting in the waiting room, huddled together consoling each other. Mr. Andersen was the first to notice him.

"Finn, you're here. We were waiting until we heard more before calling you," he said solemnly.

"I went over to the bakery this morning to pick Sally and

Nora up for church. I couldn't believe the building was on fire. Tom told me they brought the women here."

"It's bad, Finn," Mrs. Andersen said, as she reached for Finn's arm to steady herself. Sally suffered smoke inhalation and burns. Nora's in a coma." Her eyes filled with tears as she spoke.

Finn sat with the Andersens, staring at the double doors leading into the treatment rooms. He had the urge to bust right through them and find Sally. He had to see her for himself and know that she was safe. He knew he couldn't do that, but he had to do something with his nervous energy. He left to find the cafeteria and get coffee for everyone. It was going to be a long day.

Just as he returned, Dr. Turley, the attending physician in the ER, joined them to provide updates. "I understand both women were together on the third floor of a building. Is that correct."

"Yes, sir," Finn responded. "How are they?"

"They both suffered severe smoke inhalation. Sally's suffered some burns. Right now, we're giving her fluids and oxygen. We're treating the burns to prevent infection. She's in pain so we're giving her medication for that, too."

"Can we see her?" Mrs. Andersen asked eagerly.

"I want to give her some more time to adjust to the treatments we're giving her before sending in visitors. You need to understand, she won't be able to talk for a while. Her throat is severely irritated and she's short of breath. The burns aren't the worst I've seen, but she's going to need some patience and understanding because she's going to have scars. That can be alarming to a young woman. Let's let her rest and I'll check back in a couple hours and see how she is. It might be okay then to go in for a few minutes. You'll have to wear a mask and gown. We can't risk any chance of infection."

"What about Nora?" Mr. Andersen asked.

THE SKETCH

"Nora's in a coma. It seems the smoke inhalation affected her more deeply. She must have been in a different part of the apartment than Sally. We didn't find any burns, but what she suffered from the smoke was bad. The body has a way of shutting down when it can't handle any more. We're doing all we can to give her fluids and oxygen, and we've got her on a monitor, so we'll know the minute she wakes up."

"Doctor, is there a chance she won't wake up?" Mrs. Andersen asked, her frail voice fading.

"The longer she's in the coma, the more concerned we'll be. I'd say let's hold off for now on making any predictions. You'll be able to go in and sit with her once we move her out of the ER. I believe familiar voices around people in comas can help. If you're praying people, the chapel is on the fifth floor. If you need anything at all, just ask the nurses. Both girls will be moved up to ICU shortly, so we can monitor them more closely. When we do that, we'll let you know. There's a waiting room up there you'll be able to use."

"Thank you, doctor," they each mumbled, processing what they'd been told. Dr. Turley turned and left, going back through the looming double doors that separated them from their loved ones.

The Andersens headed to the chapel to pray, leaving Finn to his own thoughts. *How could this happen? Was it just a random accident or did this have to do with her searching for information about that boy she found? How would anyone even know she was searching and what she found? We finally got back together after being apart for so long. She has to be okay.* Finn pushed aside the spiraling ideas rushing at him. Sitting alone was going to make him crazy. He had to do something constructive. He pulled out his phone to notify Jen and their other friends. His last call was to Mike.

Mike's tone was serious. "What can I do to help you, Finn?"

"Last night, I sent off my preliminary plans to the architects on the fourth floor and asked them to draw up the blueprints for the barn and the rest of the farm renovations we have planned. Can you follow up with them to get that done? I could really use your help to get these permits I need to move forward. It sounds like Sally will have a stretch of recovery ahead of her and I plan to be beside her every step of the way. I need to know that barn will be ready for our Christmas wedding."

"You got it. Anything else?"

Staring out the window, Finn swallowed hard and blinked back tears before he could speak again. "Mike, I keep wondering what I would do if something worse had happened to her? She has to come through this."

"Have faith. I'll be praying for you both."

"Thanks, Mike. You're a good friend."

An hour later, the Andersens returned, followed by a nurse who informed them the women were being moved upstairs. Entering the ICU unit, they were struck by the bright lights, sterile white walls, and medicinal smell of bleach and floor cleaner. The waiting area was a bit more pleasant with comfortable chairs, a kitchenette, and magazines. The head ICU nurse assured them, "Your daughters are going to be well cared for."

It wasn't long before Tom came through the door and joined them.

"I looked for you downstairs. They sent me up here."

"Do we know anything yet about how this happened?" Finn asked.

"It's too early to say. Look, the investigation's going to take time. In fact, that's why I'm here. I'd like to talk to the women if I can."

"That's not possible. Nora's in a coma and Sally can't talk, never mind barely breathe on her own. They have both of them on oxygen and fluids and meds and they're treating Sally's burns."

Finn pulled Tom out of earshot from Sally's parents. "There's something you should know. I don't know if anything will come of this, but Sally was going to call you tomorrow when she thought you'd be back in town."

"What about?"

"Sally went through her computer the other night and found some searches in her history she knows she didn't make. She also found some emails in the trash folder she thought might be spam but wasn't sure. It looks like Jimmy used her computer to find his pain killers after all. I told her to wait until you got back into town and not to tell anyone in the meantime. Now I wish I hadn't told her that and she reported it right away. Think it's all related?"

"I'm starting to think it is. I saw Doc Johnson this morning. When he heard about the fire at Sally's, he got worried and stopped by the scene hoping to catch me. Finn, Goldie was poisoned."

"Boss, we only meant to torch the computer so they couldn't get any info from them, but the fire got out of hand fast. We barely got out of there ourselves. Besides, it's all for the best. The girl knew too much anyways. For sure, she was going to go to the cops. I doubt she'll remember anything she might have seen now."

"No one was supposed to die. It just brings more cops around. This is on you, Vic, and your crew. I'm not taking the fall for you messing up. You need to make sure that girl doesn't remember anything – whatever it takes."

"Listen, Boss, we got supplies coming in and a shipment

ready to go out tonight. The pill pressers have been working around the clock. Everything's still on-track."

"Not everything. I want that land next door so we can increase production. I've got pressure on me too, you know. Pay a visit to our lawyer friend and remind him who's paying his bills."

EIGHT

The next day Finn stopped on Main Street on his way to visit Sally. He just had to see the site of the fire again. He pulled in as near to the area as he could, surprised to see the site cordoned-off by fencing. Smoke rose out of the debris and an acrid fog hung in the air. The mix of toxic plastic and wood fumes overwhelmed him. Becoming nauseous, he hopped back in his Jeep and headed to the hospital.

He arrived in time to see a nurse escorting Tom into Sally's room. *Is she up for questions? What's Tom after?* he asked himself. He wanted to protect Sally in her frail condition, but after viewing the building site this morning, he understood the need to find out how the fire started. He had to hold himself back from following Tom into the room, afraid his presence and own questions would overwhelm her.

Tom looked down at Sally lying in the bed with her eyes closed. A sheet covered her from her neck down. With oxygen removed, she was breathing on her own, but IVs continued to provide nourishment and pain medicine. Sally slowly tried to open her eyes, but they only fluttered and then closed.

"It's Tom. I'm sorry this happened to you, kid. I need to find out anything you can tell me about what happened. Can you do that for me? I know it's hard to talk, so just take your time."

Sally opened her eyes and nodded, attempting to speak. "Fire... smoke... Nora. I tried to get Nora." She closed her eyes again, exhausted from the effort.

"Okay. I'm going to ask you some questions. You just nod your head. Do you know how it started? Were you cooking or something like that?"

"Sleeping," she uttered.

"Did you hear or see anything out of the ordinary before the fire or while you were trying to get out?" Sally shook her head. Already it was clear that she was exhausted from the brief visit.

"Rest now. I'll come back later and see if you remember more. You're doing good and I'm glad you'll be okay. I'll be praying for you." It appeared that Sally had already fallen back to sleep.

Finn intercepted Tom on his way out. "Did you learn anything more?"

"Not too much yet. I asked the fire chief to try to retrieve whatever he could from the rubble, but everything's burned. We still don't know if it was an accident or foul play. There'll be more of us put on the investigation to find out. How's Nora?"

"She's still in a coma. It was touch and go last night with her vitals. Father Joe stopped by to anoint her. They didn't think she'd make it. Dr. Turley says the longer she stays like this, the worse the prognosis."

In the days that followed, Finn and the Andersens alternated spending time sitting with Sally and Nora and making visits to the hospital chapel. The chapel, small and dimly lit, provided refreshing comfort from the sterile brightness of the hospital. Finn approached the front pew humbled by the magnitude of the large crucifix that hung before him.

Thank you for bringing me back to Sally. Please God, don't take her away from me now. Watch over her and help her recover. And please help Nora. Don't let her die. We all need her. She teaches us every day. Even though she lives in her own world, she reaches out to us and reminds us that it's people that matter.

Finn remembered the time he got angry at losing a football game because one of his team

mates had missed the final tie-breaking pass. He couldn't even look at the other player after the game. Later that same day, Nora showed him a picture she had drawn of him looking away from the other player with a scowl on his face. Seeing how he had treated that other player made him feel sick and prompted him to call the guy that night and make things right between them.

Oh, please God, help us as a family. And help Tom find out how this happened so no one else is hurt again.

He remained in the chapel until it was his turn to visit with Sally.

Finn shared the news of Nora's coma and Joe's death with Sally only when she asked. "I tried to get Nora. She wasn't in her bed." Sally struggled with the words, as tears trickled from her eyes.

"It's okay, Sally. I can't believe any of this is your fault." Finn tenderly reached out to gently hold her hand before continuing. "Nothing could have been left on in the kitchen that might have started the fire. You and Jen are so careful about shutting things down at night. And Nora must have gotten up for some reason and wandered. Can you remember anything else about what happened?"

Sally closed her eyes. That night flashed back before her.

She'd been dreaming peacefully, then became restless, struggling for air. As she woke, everything sounded loud around her, but she couldn't place what the noise was. She became confused. Her hands instinctively moved to her face and throat, and she felt hot sweat on her skin as she gasped for air where there was none. Thinking of Nora sleeping just on the other side of the hall, she rolled out of bed. She crawled on her hands and knees across the carpet toward the door that separated them, barely seeing through gray smoky clouds. She used her pajama sleeve to cover her hand as she reached up for the knob to pull the door open and resumed her crawl across the hall. By the time she got to Nora's room the air was so thick she couldn't see. Calling Nora's name, her voice was barely audible. She threw herself on the bed, grabbed on to an empty pile of sheets and then slipped to the floor as she passed out.

Remembering tired her. "No alarms." She coughed in spasms and closed her eyes to rest.

Finn was startled. The place had smoke detectors – so why didn't they go off? He made a mental note to call Tom to let him know. As he got up to leave, Sally reached for his hand.

"Finn," she whispered. He turned to her and leaned closer to hear her. "The doctor says I'm going to have scars."

"Oh, Sally. That's okay. You shouldn't be worried about that. You need to rest and recover."

"But scars, Finn. They'll be ugly. You need to know." Small tears fell from Sally's half-closed eyes.

"Sally, I love you. I've loved you my whole life. You are beautiful inside and out, with or without scars." Finn pressed her fingertips to his lips.

"I love you, Finn." Sally closed her eyes and fell into a deep sleep.

THE SKETCH

Later, in the waiting room, Jen arrived with sandwiches for Finn and the Andersens. They made arrangements for getting Goldie from the vet and over to Finn's house, where the dog would officially move in, since she'd be living there anyway after the wedding. Not long after, Mike arrived.

"You didn't need to drive out to Glen Rock, but I appreciate that you're here," Finn said.

"I'm here for as long as you need," Mike assured him. "I got the guys on the fourth floor to prioritize the drafts of your preliminary plans, and I brought the blueprints with me. I thought I'd make the drop-offs for you to the town officials who need them."

"I can help with that," Jen interjected. "I need something to do. I can't just sit. And I remember all the people Sally and I went to for the permits for the bakery, so we can start there." Jen hesitated before adding, "If it's alright that I help?"

"Sure," Mike agreed. "And it will give us a chance to get acquainted, since we're going to be helping our best friends get married."

"Be sure to talk to John Casey," Finn suggested, as they turned to leave. "I'm hoping he'll help. He's been our family lawyer for years and he also sits on the planning board."

"Will do!" they said in unison.

Back at Finn's farmhouse later that evening, Finn fed Goldie while Mike updated him on the progress he and Jen made. "We paid a visit to each of the members of the planning board. They appreciated getting copies of your plans and put it on the agenda for the meeting in two weeks. There'll be a public notice in the paper."

"What was the reaction?" Finn enquired.

"It was interesting. Most seemed enthusiastic for the new business. A couple were sorry the land wouldn't be farmed any longer. You might get some opposition."

"And John Casey? What did he have to say?"

"Poor guy. He looked in rough shape. Said he was in a car accident. He had a bruised face and a broken arm."

"That's horrible. He's having hard times. On top of what just happened, his wife has cancer."

"I have to tell you," Mike said, shaking his head, "he seemed ambivalent. I'm not sure he's on your side. He talked about how he liked your grandpa and wanted to help you, but he wasn't sure this was the way to develop the land. That's pretty much all he said."

"I know he has a buyer for the land, and he's been urging me to sell. I wonder if that has anything to do with it? I'd like to find out more before the meeting. I might have to go talk to him myself."

"I was thinking, maybe you want to go talk to your neighbors, too, and get them on board. It would be nice to have them on your side."

"That's a great idea, Mike. Sally mentioned they were new people. I haven't met them yet, but I'll make a point soon. So how long are you staying?"

"I'll leave at the end of the week, but I'll be back soon. I hear there's a great summer festival coming up. I plan to be here for that. You know, my grandparents had a place like this. I like it here. I'm a country boy at heart."

"You, a country boy? No way."

"Yup. I used to drive their tractor around the farm, and I loved their horses."

"And here I thought you were a city boy through and through. You have a room here at the house anytime you want it. Maybe there's a certain young woman in this town you just met, you might like to visit too?"

"Maybe," Mike winked. "You never know."

"Well, listen my friend, as much as I'd like to see you be in a relationship with Jen, don't get involved unless you're serious. Your home and job are three hours away. Jen's a great person and you're a good friend. I don't want to see either of you get hurt."

"I hear you. Right now I don't know if there's even anything there between us but I feel like my heart sings when I'm around her."

"Oh man," Finn smirked, "You got it bad."

A week later, Sally had made significant progress and was ready to be discharged from the hospital. Finn offered to pick her up and take her to her parents' home where she'd stay until the wedding. Tom stopped in to ask more questions as they prepared to leave.

"Sally, can you tell me the layout of the apartment?"

"Sure. The living room is at the front of the building. Then there's the kitchen with the door to the back stairs. Off the kitchen is a small hallway with the two bedrooms off that. Mine is in the back and the guest room Nora uses is in the front. Why is this important?"

"The fire chief says his men found you passed out against the bed in what would be Nora's room and they found Nora in the living room. We're just trying to put the pieces together."

"If Nora woke up first from the smoke, maybe she tried to get out, and then I woke after her and went to go find her. But why would she be in the living room? That doesn't make sense.

She knows where the door to the outside is. We practiced fire drills all the time. It's an old building and I always worried when she stayed over what she would do in an emergency. And why didn't the alarms go off?"

"The fire chief found cut wires. There were signs of some flammable liquids on the ground floor too. Someone intended to set a fire there."

"What? Why? Who would do that? Can we go there?" Sally's eyes went wide, and she turned to Finn. "I still can't believe I lost everything, and my sister is in serious condition. I need to see it."

"The fire chief gave his okay for you to go to the site and look through the rubble to see if there's anything that can be salvaged but one of my people or I need to escort you. We've got all the evidence needed from the site, but we don't want anyone getting hurt. And there's fencing up around the area, so we have to let you in. You're going to need work boots and gloves. I can meet you there later today if you're up to it."

"I am. Let's go."

"Hold on there, Sal," Finn objected. "You can't go rummaging through dirt and debris. You still have bandages on your burns and you're still having trouble with wheezing. I can drive you by the site to see it but then I'm taking you home to your parents' house to rest. I'll go back with Tom later and see if we can find anything worth saving."

Sally let out a sigh. "Okay, you're probably right. The doctor probably wouldn't approve either. It's only that I've missed so much already, like Joe's funeral. I need to go visit his mother at some point. And I need to figure out what to do about the bakery. The summer festival is coming up and I'll need a kitchen."

Finn embraced Sally, placing a kiss on her forehead. "All in good time, Sal. All in good time."

THE SKETCH

Finn and Tom knew as soon as they arrived site there wouldn't be much to find. The destruction had been massive. Working together to uncover pieces of charred wood, metal bedsprings, and broken pottery, their hopes were dimmed the more time they spent working at it.

Finn came across part of one of Nora's paintings, now torn and discolored, and decided to leave it. Seeing her masterpiece like that would make everyone feel worse. Tom found part of the blackboard Sally had used to advertise her pricing and he found the cash register. It was dented and empty. They filled a box with some metal pans and utensils they found but there was little else to salvage.

As they were headed out, Finn kicked what looked like a chair leg. He bent to look under it and found Nora's sketchbook. "Hey, look at this," he showed Tom. "It looks in almost perfect condition. She'll want it when she wakes up." Upon arriving home, Finn put the box along with the sketchbook in the corner of his kitchen, making a mental note to take the sketchbook to the hospital when the time was right.

NINE

Finn leashed Goldie and made his way to the farm next door. Now that Sally was home from the hospital and recovering at her parents' house, he could focus on his plans for the old farm. With the town meeting approaching, he wanted his neighbors' support with the project but wondered if he'd get it. Until he talked with them, he wouldn't know. The sun was already high in the sky, and it was warming up fast. "Are you ready to go meet our new neighbors, girl?" he asked Goldie, as she fell into a rhythmic trot next to him.

They headed down the drive and went left on the road. Finn took in the peacefulness of chirping birds and the scent of balsam fir. The grass in the fields they passed was getting tall and would need cutting soon.

Entering the drive for his neighbors' lot he noticed 'No Trespassing' signs had been posted. *Well, that's not too friendly. But maybe they're worried about hunters?* From a distance, Finn thought the property looked deserted. Curtains covered the windows and an old black van was parked at its side. He could see what looked like boxes and piles of trash behind it. The front garden looked untended and tangled and there were no welcoming chairs on the front porch which he knew was a "must have" for anyone with a farmhouse in these parts.

As they neared the house, Goldie became agitated, pulling at her leash letting out low growls.

"What is it girl? Don't worry, I'm here. We're just going to say hello to the nice people who live here." Approaching the front door, he rang the bell.

Down in the basement of the farmhouse, the two men, who'd been working side by side, were alerted by the security cameras on the wall.

"I'll go," Vic said, turning to Nikolai. "You watch the monitors."

"I will. Looks like the guy's got a dog with him but I don't see any car. Maybe it's just someone lost or selling something." Vic headed up the stairs after removing his apron and face mask. He made his way to the front of the house tucking in his shirt and stopping long enough at the mirror to put his hand through his hair.

"Hey. What's up?" Vic asked cooly, as he pulled the door open only enough to show half his face. "We're not buying anything."

"Hi, I'm Finn. I'm not selling anything. And this is Goldie. I'm your neighbor next door."

"What do you want?"

"I just wanted to introduce myself and tell you a little about some changes I want to make to my land. I'm planning some renovations and there'll be a town planning meeting coming up. I'm hoping for your support." Goldie let out another low growl and hung her head. "What did you say your name was?"

"I didn't."

"Oh, yeah, um…what is it, Goldie?" Finn said, turning to the anxious dog. "Sorry. I don't know what's gotten into her.

She's not usually like this." Goldie pulled on her leash attempting to back away. "Well, I wanted to talk to you about my plans but maybe this isn't a good time."

"No, it's not. I'm pretty busy, but thanks," Vic said closing the door shut.

Finn was taken aback by the encounter. *People in these parts are usually more friendly. Maybe it was just a bad time for an unexpected visit. And what's got into this dog? What's she so afraid of?*

They headed back down the hill the way they came, Goldie easing up on her aggression as they went. Approaching his house, Finn released Goldie off her leash, and she ran right to the door. Once inside she went to her bowl of water and drank in long, hard gulps.

Finn took out his laptop to pull up the local real estate records, as the dog finally snuggled down at his feet. He wanted to know more about his neighbor. A few clicks got him to the tax rolls where he found the property was owned by an LLC. A more clicks and he found the LLC was based out of Boston. He looked up the public notices about the sale and found that his attorney, John Casey, had facilitated the deal. *Hmmm. That's interesting,* he thought.

Looking up from his laptop, he glanced at the TV he'd put on earlier to catch the latest local news. A few reporters had gathered in front of what used to be Sally's bakery. He turned the volume up to listen closer.

"Good morning! This is Laura Bristol of KGRK news. We're here at the site of The Bread Basket, the former bakery owned by Sally Andersen, a native of Glen Rock. Neighbors in this town are still looking for answers as to what caused the fire that destroyed this three-story building in the heart of downtown Glen Rock a few weeks ago. They're also wondering when cleanup of the site will begin. The fire that tore through this building killed one tenant and injured both the owner and her sister, who is still in a coma at City Hospital.

"Sally, the owner of the bakery, you may remember, is the person who found Jimmy Dalton, a high school senior, dead on the trail behind the school. We've learned Jimmy's death was most likely an accidental drug overdose. The medical examiner on the case found Percocet and fentanyl in his system. Neighbors are wondering if the two incidents are related. We got no reply from either the police chief or the fire chief when we reached out to them, but we did learn from the mayor that the cleanup of the site behind me will be on the agenda for the next town meeting along with some other projects being proposed for the town. Next up we'll be talking to the mayor about this year's upcoming summer festival, so stay tuned."

Finn rose to turn off the television before the station broke to a commercial. It was time to go visit Mr. Casey and press for some answers.

"Look, Finn. You know I can't divulge information about any of my clients, even if it's just real estate." The lawyer looked tired but his response to Finn's visiting had been gruff. There wasn't going to be any small talk today.

"I'm just trying to find out who my neighbor *is*, John."

"And I wish I could help you, but I can't."

"Okay then, tell me more about this prospective buyer for my land." Finn thought changing the subject a little might soften the lawyer and bring his original question back around full circle.

"All I can tell you is he's making a great offer for the land. He's willing to double the original offer. I don't think you're going to do better than that. I saw the plans you want to present to the town. What this guy is willing to pay you is more than you'll make off your new business in a lifetime. Why not take the deal and buy something else for your project?"

"John, I'm surprised you would suggest that. You know that land has been in my family for generations. No way can I sell it, especially now that Sally and I are going to be married." Finn's anger at getting the runaround was starting to flare. "You told me it was an outside firm from Boston. Is it the same firm that bought my neighbor's land?"

"Like I said, I can't give out client information. I'm sorry." John stood up, indicating the visit with Finn was over.

"And you're not going to support my proposal for the event venue, are you?" Finn asked, already having given up hope.

"Probably not. It's my job as a member of the planning board to look out for what's best for the community. I think your plan will bring too much traffic to that part of town. The people who are out there want peace and quiet. You won't be able to change my mind."

Finn left his lawyer's office distraught. He didn't understand the change in their family friend.

Finn picked up Goldie from the house and headed to the park to take a walk and think. The recent events played in his head over and over again but brought no new conclusions. On his way home, he decided to stop in at the police station and see if Tom was around. Walking into the station, he was hit by the smell of stale coffee.

"Can I help you?" a woman officer Finn hadn't recognized asked.

"Yes, is Tom here?"

"Who should I say is asking?"

"Finn Webster."

The woman picked up her phone and said a few muffled words into the handset. While Finn waited, he noticed a box of what looked like three-day old donuts sitting alongside the offending coffee on a table behind the reception desk. *We better get Sally back to baking soon or the police station, if not the whole town is gonna fall apart*, he thought to himself with a half laugh.

Tom came out to greet Finn and noticed him eyeing the stale coffee and donuts. "I know, we got to get Sally's bakery up and running again. And now we got a new receptionist while Jeanie's out on maternity leave. Too much change for me all at once."

Heading back to the chief's office, Finn asked, "Any updates yet?"

"Not really. Seems like things are at a standstill. We know the fire was set, but not much else."

"Tom, I'm worried about Sally. She found something on her computer and then the place burned down. That can't be a coincidence. And we still don't know how anyone knew she found those suspicious emails."

"The DEA is involved now. We're working it as a three-prong investigation with us and the fire marshal. I can't really say more than that."

"Do you think Sally's in danger? I mean if the people who did this, did it because they thought she knew something, then what's to stop them from doing something again?"

"We're increasing patrols in her parents' neighborhood. Without more to go on, there isn't much we can do."

"Well, that's something, anyways."

"How's Nora?" Tom asked with concern.

"No change. Still in a coma."

"That's rough. Look, I'll try to keep you up to speed on the investigation when I can but for now why don't you and Sally get to work on your plans. I hear you're going to get some big renovations underway, and Sally's got to find a place to set up so she can get back to work." He smiled. "Tell her we need those muffins she makes."

"Joe's mother has offered to let Sally use the kitchen at the diner in the afternoons after they close up for the day. And she can use it all day on Mondays when they're closed. That'll at least give her some place to get started back up. I'll let you get back to work. You'll be at the town planning meeting this week?"

"Me and the whole town."

The sign on the outside door had the name of a real estate firm printed in big gold letters, and the front office had four realtors working behind cubicles on what appeared to be local area listings. But the partners who were meeting in the back office covered territory all over the country, and they weren't realtors.

"Listen boys," Rodney began. "We're set to increase production on all fronts. Demand is up and that means we gotta get more supply out. More supply means more profits. If we're all in agreement, I want to expand into new products like nasal spray and gummies."

The partners all nodded their agreement.

"And get the word out to your crews. Make the appropriate accommodations. We got a lot of powder coming in the next couple weeks and no shortage of labor. Expansion's underway. Questions?" Rodney sat back, pleased there seemed to be enthusiasm amongst the group.

"Yeah, I got one," Max, who'd been silent up to now chimed in. Before going on, he filled a crystal cut, high ball glass for each man, from the bottle of bourbon sitting on Rodney's desk.

As he passed them around, he continued, "What's going on in Glen Rock? Are your boys there going to be okay? Seems like there's a lot going on down there that could put us all in jeopardy."

"It's under control," Rodney grumbled in his low deep voice. "Some of the product got out a little too close to home. We've got guys working on covering up the last few little details." Rodney took a sip from his drink. The bourbon was smooth and went down warm. He sat back feeling more than slightly worried that his pending land deal wouldn't go through and about the woman in Glen Rock who might still know too much.

TEN

Sally was eager to get back to baking. It was a good distraction from thinking about her sister in the hospital and the fire. *I'll always have these scars on my body,* she thought as she pulled her sleeves lower over her wrists. Through the cotton of her blouse, she could feel the protective bandages still wrapped around her forearms. Her jeans chaffed against the bandages remaining on her legs. *These will haunt me forever and never let me forget what happened.* She felt a moment of overwhelming sadness before taking a deep breath to reign in her thoughts.

Noticing that Jen was working at a pace faster than she was, Sally took another deep breath and refocused on her work. She had always donated baked goods for the town meetings and that night's meeting was not going to be an exception, despite her still feeling fatigued from her trauma. Mixing cookie dough, she turned her thoughts to Finn and wondered if there'd be any opposition to the plans for his property.

"It was great that Joe's mom was willing to let you use the diner," Jen commented as she placed the first batches of cookies in the kitchen's massive oven. "We should be able to make enough cookies to fill at least one table in the back tonight."

"Everyone in town's been great," Sally agreed. "The insurance company's been notified about my place, but it's going to be some time before the place can be rebuilt. I might have to look for other options but for now, this is better than nothing. We'll need to pace the number of orders we take. And, after tonight we've got the summer festival to bake for. The weekend's coming fast."

"I heard Mike's coming for that," Jen said, sounding hopeful.

"That's what he said. He told Finn he's a country boy after all. And I think he might have made a new friend here during his last visit." Sally looked for a reaction from her friend.

"I wonder who that could be?" Jen smiled shyly.

Before Sally could tease her friend more, there was a loud knock at the front door of the diner. Sally left the kitchen to find Tom looking through the windows with cupped hands shielding the afternoon sun's glare.

"Hi, what are you doing here?" Sally asked, surprised as she unlocked the door and let him in.

"I heard you were using the kitchen here. I just wanted to ask you if you remembered anything more from the fire or from the search you did on your computer that night."

"Honestly, I've been trying not to think about it. Some parts of the events surrounding the fire keep coming back to me in nightmares and other parts are a blank. I'm sorry, I wish I could remember more," Sally said with sincerity.

"Okay. The DEA is sending in an agent on the weekend, and he'll want to talk to you. They're hoping with some suggestions you'll be able to remember more of those emails and the sites you found that Jimmy had visited on your computer. One of them could be the link we're looking for. He'll show you some logos and pictures and that might trigger something. Right now, you're our only hope. Are you up for that?"

Sally sighed. "We have the summer festival this weekend. Can it wait until Monday? I'll be more relaxed, and my head will be clearer when that's over."

"I think so. Don't worry. Mm. It sure smells good in here. This is all for tonight's meeting? You know it's going to be a full house."

"That's what I heard. We'll see you there."

By six forty-five the town hall was packed. Finn had gotten there early so he could greet people in hopes that a smile and a handshake would help win approval for his project. It looked like most of the town was in attendance, including a few news reporters. As he was about to take his seat with Sally, he noticed two men come in and take seats in the back. He didn't know them. One was wearing a suit which was a bit overdressed for the Glen Rock people, but the other's flannel shirt blended right in. He leaned towards Sally and asked, "Who are those guys in the back?"

Sally looked over her shoulder and at first didn't notice who Finn meant. Then she saw them staring at her and she quickly turned back in her seat. "I don't know. One of them looks a little familiar, like maybe from the bakery. But not the other. Maybe they're just new in town." Sally shrugged and added, "There's a few other people here I don't know either. Most look like they might be from outlying farms."

Pete Griswald, who Finn remembered as his high school chemistry teacher, was now head of the town board. His gavel came down hard on the wooden table, hushing the crowd. "This meeting's called to order. We have a lot to get to and a full house tonight. We're making an adjustment with the standard agenda and we're going to ask Tom Bashill, our fine police chief to say a few words to us about some of the events that have been happening around town. Tom, would you like to come up?"

Tom stepped up to the platform and adjusted the microphone towards him. "Good evening, everyone." The microphone squealed, causing groans from the crowd. After some minor adjustment, he continued. "It's good to see such a large turnout tonight. I want to speak about a few things that some might find upsetting, but I feel as the police chief, it's my duty to bring out in the open. Folks, we've all been hearing on the news about the opioid crisis in this country. They're calling it an epidemic, though up to now we haven't seen much in these parts. The number of people dying from the misuse and overuse of drugs every day is rising to astounding numbers. Over 150 people die every day in this country from overdoses related to synthetic opioids like fentanyl, which is fifty times stronger than heroin and one hundred times stronger than morphine. Walking through our quiet peaceful community you might think our small town is immune to something like this. We're not.

"In the last month alone, there have been no fewer than twenty overdoses in the tri-county area. And we've seen it right here in Glen Rock, too. What I want to say to you tonight is that we are committed to doing everything we can to protect the good people of our community so we're going to work with the city leaders, the school counselors, and community services through the hospital to form a task force and look at things like available mental health services and other supports. You'll hear more about that another time from people who can address that better than me."

Josh McKenna, the owner of the local grocery store, stood up from his seat in the third row. "Chief, if I can interrupt, aren't some towns installing Narcan stations around so people can help if there's an overdose? Is that kind of thing necessary here, or does it just encourage more drug use?"

Tom nodded, indicating he heard the man. "That's a great question. Every member of our police force and the fire department has been trained in the use of Narcan and will now carry it with them and be ready if called to administer it. We're also installing Narcan stations at key locations in the community including the library, the courthouse, the hardware store, and more places to be named soon. These stations can be easily accessed by anyone who needs to assist someone who's overdosed as the result of consuming substances such as heroin, fentanyl, or prescription medications. We don't' think it will encourage drug use, and it can save lives. We'll provide workshops and training for those interested, but there are directions in each of the kits, which contain two doses."

Tom paused a moment before continuing. "Folks, the drugs on the streets today aren't the same drugs we used to find. There are all kinds of counterfeit pills out there and they're easy enough to access through illegal online pharmacies. Parents, I've said it before, know what your kids are doing online and with social media. We all need to pay attention. We're all responsible for our kids and each other. As a community and working with others in our neighboring towns, we can come together around this problem and spread the safety net that's needed to curb these terrible drugs invading our tri-county area. They'll be more to come. I just wanted to give you a heads up on the state of things. Thank you."

Tom sat down noting the room's hush had turned to a low and somber murmuring. Pete tapped his gavel again bringing order back to the meeting. "Next we want to hear about where things are with the summer festival."

Dolly Benson, a stout young woman Finn didn't recognize, stood, and went to the front. "We're all set for the weekend. The roads in the area will be closing tomorrow for set up. We've got music and food, and dancing, and everything you could want, and the weather looks marvelous. Can't ask for more than that."

The crowd clapped and cheered.

Finn was pleased the mood had shifted to something more positive before he was called next. "Hello, everyone. As many of you know, I'm Finn Webster. My family's farm sits outside of town off Route 52. My parents passed away about ten years ago and more recently my grandpa passed. Our land has sat quiet these last years but now I've returned to Glen Rock and I want to make something of it. I'm proposing to turn the barn and buildings into a family friendly event venue with a small brewery, restaurant, petting zoo, and a place for local vendors to show and sell their crafts. I've brought renderings of what the site will look like if I have the zoning board's approval to proceed. Tonight, I'm just here to make the initial proposal and see if there are any questions I can answer before any of this moves forward."

John Casey saw favorable nods as he looked out over the audience. Then his eyes locked on Rodney's at the back of the room. *What's he doing here? Checking up on me himself to make sure I close the property deal? His boys already reminded me what I gotta do.* Sweat broke out on his forehead as his heart began to pound. Clearing his throat, he stood to raise the first objection. "That area's always been residential and farm country. What kind of traffic is that going to bring in? Folks who live out there want quiet."

"Great question, John," said Finn. "We're going to ensure a buffer zone of trees between ourselves and our neighbors and no event will go later than midnight."

"Midnight's too late," someone from the crowd grumbled. "Us farmers rise at 4a.m., or did you forget that while you were away in the city?"

Finn couldn't make out who it was that spoke, but realized he was going to have more of a challenge than he'd expected.

By the time Pete Griswald lowered his gavel to call the meeting to a close, it was late, and Finn had answered more questions than he'd anticipated. In the end it was decided the project would need a little more study before it could proceed.

Slightly disappointed, Sally and Finn packed up the presentation posters they'd brought. Finn's phone rang. He was surprised when Mr. Andersen's name came up as the caller.

"Hello, sir."

"Hi Finn. How'd it go tonight?" Mr. Andersen asked, with genuine interest.

"Not too bad. There were a lot of questions, mostly about noise and traffic. We have some more work to do but I'm thinking positively."

"That's good. There's a lot to be thankful for. Nora's eyes began to flutter tonight, and she raised a finger. The doctors think it was more than just a spasm. We think she's waking up."

Finn couldn't believe what he was hearing. "That's great. Sally will be so excited to hear," he said enthusiastically.

"Is she around? We tried to call her, but her phone must be off. She always does that. I don't understand why she just doesn't put it on silence and vibrate," Mr. Andersen half teased.

"She doesn't want to be a slave to technology," Finn chuckled. "She's here. I'll let you tell her the good news." Finn handed the phone to Sally.

Out in the hallway, Rodney and Nikolai blended with the crowd that was leaving and followed John Casey to his car.

"Nice work, John. Keep it up," Rodney said in a low voice. "Convince the town this dream project is better in a different location, one with a nice pretty house for him to live in. And then he'll have to move. But let's not take too long."

John hesitated but then asked, "What do you want the land for anyway? Can't you use another parcel for whatever it is you have planned?"

"You ask too many questions. You're getting paid some good money to get me that land. There's no backing out now if that's what you're thinking. Do it and do it soon."

John got in his car keeping an eye on the two men as they walked towards a black Suburban parked away from the parking lot lights. When he saw them pull away, he leaned back and closed his eyes.

What have I gotten myself into? Finn and his family were friends and now I'm betraying him, and maybe the whole town.

ELEVEN

Two days later, Finn and Mike, who'd gotten into town the night before, headed over to help Sally and Jen move their baked goods from the diner to the fairgrounds. Sally was bubbling over with excitement. Her sister had finally woken up and it was the first day of the summer festival. They were all excited to be doing something fun after all the drama of the last weeks.

Sally and Jen had been baking nonstop in preparation of the big weekend. "Between what we put in my Jeep, your Blazer, and the bakery's van, we have enough goodies to satisfy every sweet tooth in the entire town," Finn teased.

When they arrived at the fairgrounds most of the townspeople were already milling around making last-minute preparations and by noon, the fun was in full swing. A voice came over the loudspeaker to announce the opening with the singing of "The Star-Spangled Banner" which was followed by cheers from the crowd.

Feeling the excitement of the day, Finn and Mike were quick to go off to try their strength at ax throwing and to check out the new line of John Deere tractor equipment with promises to return to Sally and Jen in time to get dinner from the Chicken Shack stand, dance under the stars to the sounds of McElroy's Country Western Band, and watch fireworks at midnight.

Sally and Jen worked their booth, which had no end of customers. Between filling orders and greeting people, Sally couldn't stop humming.

"It's good to see you so happy, girlfriend," Jen said, smiling.

"I am. Truth be told, though, I'm also a little worn out. Maybe I'm just tired from so much baking and the pressure to get everything done in time. But mostly, of course, I'm so happy that Nora is recovering."

"I'm sure having your sister in the hospital, and the fire, and Jimmy's death – well, all of it has to have been exhausting. I can't pretend to know what it's like, but you have every right to be tired in my book."

Sally nodded. "And I'm having nightmares about the fire and flashbacks about that night. I'm starting to remember things. Just bits and pieces. It's like it's all just beyond my reach."

"Well, Monday when you meet with the DEA, they'll be able to help you get at it and then maybe you won't have to think about it all the time anymore. Listen, if you need to take a break or even want to go home and take a nap at any point, I'm fine here. You just go."

"No way! We're going to have fun today," Sally insisted, flashing a smile.

Sally and Jen worked until a shift of people who had been temporarily hired for the event came, freeing them up to go find their dates. After walking the grounds for a while, they found the men in line for the logging competition.

"Oh, this should be fun to watch," Sally teased.

"I've got to get my camera out for this," Jen joked. "What's next for them, bull riding?"

Finn and Mike took turns rolling the logs under their feet in the shallow pond set up for the event. Both men and the crowd they'd drawn to watch laughed hysterically when they fell off. It was clear they weren't going to win this event. After several tries, they finally gave up and went to dry off by their friends who'd been watching from behind the fencing.

After checking out the sheep shearing, the chainsaw wood carving, and walking through the vendor booths, they headed over to the arcades where Mike won Jen a stuffed bear for knocking over bottles with a baseball. Rides on the Ferris wheel, merry go round, and finally the Hill Flyer, a giant roller coaster, left them all hungry and they made the food court their next stop.

Finn was overwhelmed by how many people stopped him to welcome him back to town and to congratulate him and Sally on their engagement. Many of them offered Sally kind words about her sister, about Joe's death, and the fire. Others had been at the town meeting and wished them luck on their event venue proposal.

Later when they danced to the songs of Merle Haggard and Loretta Lynn, Sally rested her head on Finn's shoulder and let him hold her close. She was feeling tired but relaxed for the first time in weeks. Mike and Jen danced next to them.

"Are you having fun?" Mike asked softly.

"I am," Jen said, and then added thoughtfully, "It's amazing there are so many stars out tonight and I just love this festival. Everyone's so happy. Are you having a good time?"

"Best night ever!" he exclaimed, grinning ear to ear, pulling her a little closer.

As the night grew late, people began to rally around for the long, anticipated fireworks show. The four friends found a spot midway in the bleachers, not far from Tom and Debbie and several other people they knew.

Sally turned to Finn. "I'm just going to head over to the

ladies' room and stop to make sure our booth's closed up tight for the night."

"Okay, I'll come with you," Finn offered.

"No. You stay here with our friends. I'll be back before the fireworks start." She kissed him and slipped away before he could object.

Sally crossed the open field where they'd played games earlier in the day. She felt the cool evening breeze caress her cheek. *I'm one lucky girl,* she thought. *I'm in love with my best friend and I'm getting married. And now Nora's recovering. Wow! I'm so blessed. Things have been rough but so many of my dreams are coming true.*

Sally finished up in the ladies' room and headed towards her booth beyond the fields near the main entrance. Strung up lights lit the path, giving the looming shadows a golden glow. It was quiet at that end of the park except for one or two vendors who were still packing up for the night. Her breath caught in her throat, startled by what sounded like the lid of a tin can falling over behind her in one of the stalls. *Oh stop, silly girl. You spook too easily. It's just a cat or something. Get a grip.*

Instinctively, she reached to her back pocket to grab her phone. *I'll call Finn and let him know I'll just be another few minutes.* But the phone wasn't there. She tried to remember where she might have left it. Bewildered, she thought, *Maybe the Chicken Shack, or maybe it fell out of my pocket on the roller coaster or climbing up the bleachers. Ugh! It's a new phone, too.*

Approaching her booth, Sally was surprised the string of lights around her section were out. Although it was dark, she knew her way from the many years of attending the festival. *I just need to make sure the booth is locked,* she told herself.

Reaching for the knob to the door, she smelled something funny as an arm came from behind and a hand covered her face. She heard the first of the fireworks go off as she grew dizzy and weak before collapsing in her captor's arms.

TWELVE

Finn glanced at his watch as the stadium lights went off and the first fireworks shot up.

Sally should have been back by now. I should have gone with her. What was I thinking letting her go off on her own? Where is she?

He scanned the cheering crowd that had spilled out from the bleachers to the grassy area around the stadium. Darkness kept him from seeing anything more than an outline of the large crowd of people and the glow wands children waved in play. Pulling out his phone, he dialed Sally's number. There was no answer.

"I'm going to look for her," Finn said, turning to his friends.

"Do you want us to come with you?" Mike offered.

"No, thanks. You stay and enjoy the show. Save our seats. I'm sure she's on her way back. With the lights off everywhere, it's dark. I just want to go meet her so she doesn't have to make the walk back alone."

Finn left the bleachers under a sparkling sky and headed towards the fields past where the games had been played earlier in the day. Beyond those were the vendor sheds. The vastness of the park was magnified by the darkness, broken only intermittently, by the light show overhead. Finn realized there were several paths Sally could have taken. He chose what he hoped would be the most direct. The further from the crowd he went, the more the silence of the night and an uneasiness grew in his gut.

The fields were empty and from a distance he could see there were no signs of anyone near the vendor shacks. Everyone had shut down their stalls for the night. As he drew closer, it was clear the bakery shed was deserted.

"Sally! Sally! Are you here?"

His calls were met by silence.

Sally, where are you? Somewhere out in this field without a flashlight and probably either without your phone or you've turned it off again. I walked the most direct route. How could I have missed seeing you?

Finn retraced his steps, calling out her name as he went. Stopping by the dimly lit women's bathrooms he leaned in and called her name. There was no answer. Making his way back toward the bleachers he wondered if she hadn't already returned, and he'd just missed her in the dark. The thought quickened his steps in hopeful eagerness. Disappointment and a pang of anxiety stopped him when he neared his friends and saw she still wasn't there.

"Sally didn't come back?" Finn asked frantically, already knowing the answer.

"No," Mike answered. "Is everything alright?"

"I'm not sure," Finn said with worry. "I couldn't find her."

"She knows we're here, so she'll just come back when she's done with whatever she had to take care of," Mike said, trying to reassure his friend.

"Maybe," Finn shouted over the whistle of the fireworks

shooting up. "But I couldn't find her anywhere and now my gut is telling me something's not right."

Mike could see the worry in Finn's eyes. He leaned in to Jen to explain what was going on. Jen jumped up, grabbing her sweater as she stood.

"Come on. Let's go look for her together," Jen said gesturing that they go.

Tom noticed the three friends leaving before the finale and guessed that something wasn't right. Leaving Debbie, he headed down the bleachers behind them to catch up.

"Hey! What's going on, guys? Why are you leaving?" Tom asked.

"We're going to look for Sally," Finn said, his distress evident. "She went to check on her booth and never came back. She's not answering her phone and I went to look for her but couldn't find her. So now we're all going to look."

"I'm sure she's around. Maybe she had to take some things to the car. Did you try the parking lot?" Tom suggested.

"No, we'll try there. You're probably right. She's here someplace. Hey, if you see her would you have her call me?" Finn asked feeling reassured that Sally might be in the one place he hadn't looked.

"Of course. I need to get back to Debbie, but text me when you catch up with Sally just so I know everything's okay."

The three friends headed back through the fields, past the vendor booths, and out to the parking lot, calling Sally's name. The fireworks finale burst with red, white, and blue sizzles and pops overhead.

Sally struggled to clear her way free of the weight that wanted to pull her deeper into a dark hole. Waking slowly, the insides of her head were spinning as growing panic filled her mind. Rolling onto her side, she could neither move her arms or her legs. Pain wrapped itself around them as she tried to free herself from whatever had them bound. The gag in her mouth held back the scream she was desperate to cry out. Panic overtook her as tears fell from her covered eyes and she remembered her last moments awake.

I was about to enter the shed to check on things. Now I'm here. Where's here? That smell. What is that? Ugh!

Pungent rot filled her nostrils through the bristled fabric that covered her head. She tried to sit up but was still too weak and dizzy. Losing her balance, she fell back on her side. Whatever she was lying on was fairly soft, shifting underneath her as she moved. Outside mumbled voices seemed to be moving farther away.

"Why'd you bring her here?" a man asked in a low voice.

"Only way we can keep an eye on her until the boss tells us what to do next," another man, with a deeper voice, answered. "She ain't getting away tonight. I got her tied up pretty good."

"If that's what the boss wants."

"Yeah. Let's get inside. I could use a beer."

Sally lay there in silence, trying to calm herself, regain her strength, and gather her wits. She began to pray.

———

Finn's heart raced as the three friends approached the parking lot. Calling out Sally's name, they saw no signs of her. Their cars were all parked where they had left them, and a quick inspection showed that nothing looked touched or out of place. In the distance they heard the crowd cheering the end of the fireworks show and they knew the large group of attendees would soon be descending on the lot. The three friends stood staring out over the festival site, not knowing what to do next when Finn's phone rang.

"Did you find her?" Tom shouted over the noise of the crowd.

"No. It's like she disappeared," Finn said in an anxious voice.

"Okay. Debbie's sister is going to take her home. I'm on my way to you. Meet me at the bakery's shed. And Finn, don't worry. We'll find her," Tom reassured, though he felt just as anxious as his friend.

Minutes later, Tom directed his questions to the group. "So, she left the stands about ten minutes before the fireworks started? And she was just going to the women's bathroom and then to make sure the shed was locked up?"

"Yeah. When the fireworks started, I came to look for her. When I couldn't find her, I headed back to the bleaches thinking we may have been on different paths. You know the rest of the story," Finn said, rubbing the back of his neck to relieve the tension growing there.

"And she's not answering her phone?" Tom asked.

"No. She sometimes doesn't leave it on. I should have gone with her. I don't know what I was thinking." Finn lamented.

"Beating yourself up won't help. Let's focus," Tom said, taking charge. "I've called the maintenance guys to get more lights on over here and asked them to get me their keys for the sheds. I'm going to ask security to check all the bathrooms. You three stay together here while I check on a few other things," he commanded as he turned to make some calls on his cell phone.

It wasn't long before flood lights popped on throughout the site and more police arrived on the scene.

Tom barked his orders. "Okay, people, we're looking for a thirty-year-old woman, 5'7", long brown hair. Her name's Sally Andersen. She was last seen leaving the bleachers and headed in this direction. She was wearing jeans, a plaid shirt, navy blue sweater, and work boots. We're looking for any clues that might help us. If you find any lost items, bag them, and mark their location. Go in pairs and spread out. There's a lot of area to cover. We're going to do a search of the entire grounds and the outside perimeter of the park. Check behind and inside every shed and outbuilding. Call out if you find something – anything."

The crowd of festival goers was thinning but those who lingered heard what was going on. Pete Griswald was among them. "Can we help, Chief?"

"Yes," Tom said waving him to join him. "Find a few good people and make a search party. We're looking for Sally. If anybody finds anything, have them call out. Under no circumstances do they touch anything."

"On it, Chief. Don't worry. We'll find her," Pete said, glancing at Finn, who looked shaken and worn.

Minutes passed like hours and Jen approached Finn with reassuring words. "We're all praying they find her. You just need to trust."

Finn was about to thank her when Tom's radio beeped. "Chief! We got something over here! Behind the shed."

"Clear the area. Everyone get back," Tom shouted, turning his attention to his officer.

"Looks like the dirt's all scuffed here by the door. And there's two drag marks back into the trees," the officer pointed out.

"No, no, no," Finn cried out racing to follow Tom.

"Finn, get back. You don't want to destroy any clues or evidence," Tom said, physically pushing Finn back several steps. "Look, we don't know what it means until we can get a forensics team out here. And we're still going to search the entire area. This might not be what you think it looks like."

"She's gone, Tom. Someone took her. I know it." Finn didn't

want to believe his own words. "How could I be so stupid to let her go on her own?"

"Mike," Tom called out. "Take Finn home. Listen, the three of you need to go. Let us do our work. When we're done here, I'll come to the house and if we need something from you in the meantime, I'll know where to find you."

Tom turned to his team. "Get this area taped off. This is officially a crime scene."

THIRTEEN

The next morning the three friends joined the Andersens at the early Sunday Mass. None of them had slept after sharing the news of Sally's disappearance with her parents but agreed that going to Mass would at least bring some comfort. Before giving the final blessing, Father Joe announced that coffee and sandwiches would be available in the Social Hall at noon for any members of the police force or the community who needed a respite from the search for one of their own members of the parish.

"I'll be available to anyone needing spiritual comfort or wanting to pray for Sally's safety," Father Joe concluded. "Our prayers of course go out to all of Sally's friends and family."

Exiting the church, Finn noticed Tom standing at the back, gesturing them aside as they approached. "Before you go out there, you need to know that members of the press have gathered. Someone must have heard our call on the scanner to get more officers on the scene. They've been following me like pack dogs all night. We haven't provided them with any information, and they're bound to hound you."

"Shouldn't we talk to them, though? Get the word out so everyone can look for Sally?" Finn asked anxious to act.

"I want to do it orderly and there's a few things I don't want them to know." Tom spoke in a lowered voice in the vestibule of the now-empty church.

"Like what?" Finn pleaded. "What have you found?"

"Not now, Finn. There'll be time to talk later down at the station. We're going to call a press conference at eleven-thirty. That will get the story on the noon news and give you a couple hours to get some coffee and prepare yourselves. Finn and Mr. and Mrs. Andersen, I'd like you to speak. Go home now and come to the station at eleven. Millie from my office will help you with what to say. Michelle Jacobs from the Missing Persons Task Force will be there and my contact from the DEA who was going to arrive tomorrow is coming in early for it. They'll want to talk to you all after."

"This is all a little overwhelming for us," Mr. Andersen said in an exhausted, weakening voice. "And we need to get to the hospital to be with Nora. She's only just come around and she's scared. She can't know about any of this. Not yet."

Tom wanted to be compassionate. *These people have been through so much,* he thought, casting his eyes to the floor before making eye contact again with Mr. Andersen. "We'll try to free you up as soon as we can. Your presence at the press briefing could make a difference so I really want you there." Addressing them all, he added, "Now, we're going to have you leave by the back of the church so you can avoid the reporters. Security, what little we can spare, has been posted at your houses to make sure they don't bother you. I'll see you at the station in a bit."

Jen offered to cook breakfast for everyone back at Finn's house before heading off to the station. The smell of freshly brewed coffee and the sizzling of bacon was comforting, but little got eaten. By eleven thirty they'd regrouped at the police station and been prepped, ready for the cameras to roll.

"Good morning," Tom began. "Most of you know me. I'm Tom Bashill, chief of the Glen Rock police force. On my left I have Agent Doug Briggs of the Drug Enforcement Agency and Detective Michelle Jacobs of the Iowa Missing Persons Task Force. On my right I have Finn Webster, fiancé of our missing person, and Mr. and Mrs. Andersen, the parents of our missing woman.

"Last night at the summer festival this woman, Sally Andersen, went missing some time we believe during the fireworks show. We're getting her picture out to all of you and asking the public if they saw anything, or know anything, to please contact the police. We've set up a hotline number which we'll post at the end. We do suspect foul play in her disappearance, meaning we don't think she just took off on her own. I'd like to ask the Andersens and Finn to come up to say a few words."

Finn began with a passionate plea. "Please, if anyone has seen Sally, we need you to call. She's 5'7" and was wearing a plaid shirt and blue sweater with jeans. Please, if you know anything, call us." Mrs. Andersen broke down in tears. Covering her face, she and her husband turned away from the microphone, unable to speak.

The reporters began shouting questions. "Do we know if this is related to the bakery burning down? Is it related to that young boy she found dead? Where are you searching? What makes you think it's foul play?"

Tom stepped back to the microphone. "We're not at liberty to give out any information about our search and any ongoing investigations. We just want everyone to be on the lookout for this young woman. Thank you for coming out."

Reporters continued to shout questions as Tom ushered the three friends and Sally's parents back into the station.

Sally woke from the few minutes sleep that finally overcame her as she lay in darkness. Flapping overhead gave way to clicks and tweets. She shivered with cold, and her muscles ached from being in their cramped position for so long. Her thoughts raced as she tried to force herself to ignore the bats she sensed were fluttering over her head.

Why is this happening? One thing after another. I'm so tired. Oh Finn, after all these years, we've found each other again and now all this. Finn will know I'm missing, and he'll contact Tom. They'll all be looking for me. I just need to stay alive. They'll find me. Please God, help them to find me. Where am I? Think!

Sally opened her fingers and for the first time tried to feel what she was laying on. *The feel, the smell. Silage! It makes sense now. The dampness, the silence, bats. A silo?*

A sound behind her clipped her thoughts. She heard a door scrape open before footsteps approached and a hand grabbed her by the arm.

"Get up," the man demanded as he dragged her and put her on a hard wooden chair. Pain seared through her head as she was thrown back, hitting the concrete wall she was up against. "Now I'm going to untie your hands and tie them in front so you can eat. Don't try anything or you'll go right back on the ground. And don't scream when I take that gag out. You'll just upset my partner. You wouldn't like him upset. No one can hear you anyway. Understand?"

Sally nodded. When her hands were retied, the man put a sandwich in them. Reaching up under the hood that covered her face he removed the gag from Sally's mouth. His rough skin touching her cheek paralyzed her momentarily. His smell repulsed her. She wanted to scream but catching herself, thought it better to comply until she could think things through.

"There's a bucket on your right side next to the chair if you have to go to the bathroom."

"What do you want with me?" Sally asked hesitantly.

"The boss wants us to ask you some questions. Just tell us what he wants to know, and you'll be alright. We're not animals. We don't want to hurt you. Just do what you're told, answer the questions, and you'll be fine."

"What questions?" Sally asked.

"In time. Now eat."

"I don't want to!" Sally defied, tossing the sandwich onto the ground in front of her.

"Suit yourself. The rats will love it," the man snorted.

"Please, let me go!" Sally begged.

She sensed him walking away and the door closed with a thud. She tried to remove the hood that covered her head but couldn't. Something held it down in the back. Giving up, she tried to stand and shift her weight along the wall.

There must be a way out! The door!

"Help! Help! Can anyone hear me? Help!" Sally cried out in her weakening voice.

Sliding her feet an inch at a time, she lost her balance and fell. She pushed herself up and tried again. Facing the wall this time, she used her fingertips to help balance her weight. Fatiguing fast and making little progress, she moved back to the chair and sat. She needed to think.

The conference room at the police station was musty and dark even with the large fluorescent lights looming overhead. Tom escorted Finn inside after sending the Andersens on their way. Doug Briggs of the Drug Enforcement Agency and Michelle Jacobs of Missing Persons were already in their seats, sleeves rolled up, and laptops open in front of them.

"We just have a few questions for you," Michelle began. "If I understand correctly, you and Sally have known each other your whole lives?"

"That's right," Finn nodded.

"And while you left the area for college and lived in Des Moines after that, you recently moved back to Glen Rock and got back with Sally?"

"Yes," Finn nodded again.

Doug interrupted. "So, when Sally found the body of the dead boy, you were just getting back to town? It all happened about the same time?"

"Yes. That sounds about right," Finn answered.

"And you did some sleuthing on your own to find out how the boy might have gotten the drugs?"

"That's right," Finn stated again before going on. "He worked for Sally, so I guess that made it personal."

"And what did you find out?" Doug pursued.

"We didn't find out much. Some of his teammates confirmed they take painkillers from time to time to stay in a game, but they didn't give away much else. They told me they can get anything online but wouldn't say what sites they used. Sally found some emails in her computer the night the building burnt down but she didn't have a chance to tell anyone much about them. The last thing she said to me was that she was going to dig a little deeper. I told her to let the police do it. And then the computers were burned in the fire," Finn explained.

"I see," Doug said, sitting back in his chair without taking his eyes off Finn. "And computers were lost at the community center too."

"Yes," replied Finn. "But I don't know anything about that. Why are you asking all this?"

"We're just trying to figure out how the pieces all fit together. Doesn't it seem strange to you that you talk about checking out certain places for information and then things happen, or that Sally finds information, only tells you, and then those computers get destroyed?"

"Wait!" Finn objected, sweat forming on his forehead. "You don't think I have something to do with all this? Do I need a lawyer?"

"Finn," Tom interjected. "It's their job to look at all the evidence from every angle." Turning to the investigators he added, "Maybe we should look at what we do know, shall we?

"Sally finds a boy dead from a drug overdose. She and her friends start asking questions. The community center, where Sally asks questions and we know kids use the computers, is broken into, and the computers are damaged. Sally gets a brick thrown through her window with a note. Finn gets a brick thrown in a window at his house. That suggests someone doesn't want anyone snooping. Sally finds information on her computer. The bakery where that computer is burns down, killing Joe, one of the people asking questions, and it nearly kills Sally and her sister. So how does someone know about the questions being asked and what's been found? Someone in the circle? You can see how it looks, Finn."

"Tom, you know me. I'm not part of this. I'd never do anything to hurt Sally."

"Have you seen anyone hanging around? A stranger that's become a regular, maybe? Someone that could overhear things?" Tom persisted.

"No, no one comes to mind."

"Okay," Michelle began. "It sounds logical to think Sally was taken because she knows something about where the drugs are coming from. That narrows our window for finding her. As soon as they get what they want from her, there's no telling what they'll do. We need to get the lab to go through anything found out at the festival site as soon as possible and that includes cigarette butts found near the shed, tire tracks, anything. And have we found Sally's cell phone?"

"We found about ten cell phones at the festival site," Tom answered. "Finn, here are some photos of them. Any look like Sally's?"

"Hers could be one of these," he said pointing to one of the photos. "They all look the same but that looks like the right kind. She didn't have a case on hers yet like these. It was pretty new."

"We'll get the lab looking at these first. Do you know the password that unlocks her phone?" Tom asked picking up the photos.

"She never told me. Why is her phone important?" Finn asked.

"I think that's all the questions we have for now," Tom responded without answering the question. "We'll call you if we need anything more. You can go. I know you want to stop in to visit Nora at the hospital."

"Yeah. I want to bring her that sketchbook we found at the fire. It will help her feel better if she can draw. Keep me posted Tom. If there's anything more I can do, I want to help."

Finn drove back to his house where Mike and Jen waited for him. Goldie began barking as soon as he walked in. "Hey girl, what's got you so jumpy?"

"She's been like this," Mike said. "We took her to the park for a walk, but she can't seem to settle down. Maybe she misses Sally."

"You and me both, Goldie," Finn said snuggling his face in her fur. "You and me both."

FOURTEEN

Sally sat in silence. She was sure it was now daytime but all she saw was darkness under the hood that covered her head. *Think Sally, think. They're coming back to ask questions. What kind of information do they want? Is this about the drugs and what I found in my computer? Only Finn knew about that, and he doesn't know all of it. Oh, Finn, do they have you, too?* Sally felt her heart beat faster. Her mind was racing. *Okay, girl, you're getting carried away. Breathe. Stay alive. Escape. But how? Help me, God. Please help me with this.*

Her thoughts were interrupted by voices. She strained to hear two men talking but couldn't make out what they were saying. They were coming closer. She froze as the creaky door opened.

"Okay, princess. Here's what we're gonna do," the first man began. "We're going to ask you some questions and you're gonna answer. Then if we like your answers, we'll let you go."

"What do you want to know?" Sally asked as fear seeped through her limbs.

"Where's your cell phone?"

"I don't know." Sally's lower lip quivered.

"Wrong answer. Let's try again. Where's your phone?"

"I don't know. I must have lost it at the festival."

Sally felt the presence of the men stepping closer and her knees shook. "Give us your iCloud username and password."

"What?" Sally shrieked, not fully understanding what they were asking for.

"Your iCloud address. The thing you use to connect your accounts and devices, set up your new phone and computer. What is it?" the man with a deeper, older voice pressed on.

"I don't know it," she blurted.

"Wrong answer again. Listen, we can't help you if you don't tell us. Don't you want to go home and see your sister? Heard she just woke up at the hospital."

"Maybe we should go visit her," the other, younger sounding man said.

Fear punched Sally in the gut. *How do they know about Nora?*

"Stay away from my sister!"

"Just tell us what we want to know."

"I don't remember my address. I think the password was autogenerated or something. It was set up a long time ago. I don't remember. The store set up my new phone. I use facial recognition to log into everything. I don't know it," Sally pleaded.

"That's too bad. How about we let you think about it a little more. See what you come up with. We'll be back."

Outside the two men's voices were muffled against the cement walls that caged her. She strained to listen.

"Maybe if I go get a picture of the sister, it will scare her into telling us what we want to know," the one man said.

"Good thinking," the other man replied. "The boss is going to have us get rid of her whether she tells us or not, but he'll be a lot happier if she does."

"What's the plan?"

"We got an order of silage coming tomorrow. She'll be dead in seconds."

"Wait! I didn't sign up for that," the younger voice objected. Sally recognized it as the man who'd brought her the sandwich. "Why can't we just let her go? She didn't see us."

"She knows too much. She saw the emails and links. Seems she dug deep where most people don't go on the web. With what she knows, a good hack could trace things. Everything can be traced back to somewhere. Anyway, she's heard our voices. With reporters everywhere and the cops searching, the boss wants to move on from this mess. We get the info, and then she's done either way. Then we just lie low and get back to business as usual. We're behind on production. We got orders to fill."

Sally could taste the salt from the tears that streamed down her face. *What if they hurt Nora. I have to get to her. I have to escape. Think. I'm in a farm silo. Most silo doors only open from the outside. But there's an opening at the top for the silage. There must be metal rungs. If I could just get to them.... Impossible. Even if I could, I can't climb tied up.*

Slumping in the chair, she felt the pressure of the bindings that had her hands and ankles tied. They ate away at her raw skin. She was tired, hungry, and time was passing while she waited for whatever was going to happen next. She began to pray. *Please God, help me. I'm lost and I don't know what to do.* Her mind wandered as she began to recall the words of Psalm 27. *The Lord is my light and my salvation. Whom shall I fear... Sally don't give up. You have to try. Get up. Crawl the wall.*

Sally slid from the chair and stood facing the wall. Inching her way across the curves of the structure, and using her outstretched hands for balance, she slowly made her way. Each sidestep along the cold concrete was progress until a piece of metal bolt stabbed her hand shooting wild agony up her arm.

Warm blood oozed as she shrieked in alarm. Pulling her arm back, she nearly fell. The thunderbolt of pain left her dizzy. Kneeling on the ground she struggled to fill her lungs with air. After several deep breaths, calm reigned again. Standing cautiously, she reached in front of her to feel for the metal piece that had been her nemesis.

It's sharp. Sharp enough to cut my bindings? Try. Positioning her wrists on the knifelike metal she rubbed back and forth. Each push and pull sent a wave of pain up her hand, through to her wrist and arm. Relentless in her work, she continued until she broke free. Reaching back to pull the hood off her head she took in a deep breath and steadied herself. Seeing the blood still dripping down her shirtsleeve and on to the ground, she wrapped her wound with the hood. *It's not pretty but it will do. Okay, my ankles are next.* Sitting on the ground she worked the laces of her boot. They came undone with ease. She slipped her foot out, freeing it from the hold, and then freed the other one. *Thank you, God.*

Looking around the darkened space, Sally guessed that it was nighttime and now was her only chance to escape. Across the silo, she saw the outline of the series of bars that led up to the silage chute. Looking up at the eighty-foot wall she needed to climb caused her to momentarily doubt if she could do it. Looking around and finding no other option, she reached one arm up and then one leg at a time as she began to make her ascent.

She grit her teeth against the throbbing in her right hand each time she reached up to catch the next metal bar. A quarter way up, her foot slipped on the rusty metal. Her arm hooked the next rung down as she felt her body hurl away from the wall. Regaining her footing she started her climb again, only this time going slower. One fall meant starting over and she didn't have the time or the strength. She made a point to always hold on with her one good hand.

Finally, pulling one rung and then the next, she began to feel the air change and knew she was getting closer to the top. Forcing herself into the silage chute she knew there was only one way to go – down. Turning herself around and stretching out a leg she touched the first of the threaded rods that lined the narrow space. *You've got this girl. Keep going. Stay alive. Get to Nora.* Digging her fingertips between the raw concrete and the metal rod in front of her, she lowered herself tentatively to the next rung. Sally's heart raced as she made her descent before making a final jump to the ground.

Glancing around she could make out little under the overcast sky. She took a deep breath, filling her lungs with the first fresh air since being captured. Hearing the rustle of leaves in the light breeze, she knew her course. She ran through the open field as fast as she could towards what she hoped might be woods behind the farm.

Driven by adrenaline, she was desperate to get away. Clearing the aged three-rail fencing that separated the farmland from the woods she ran into a deeper darkness. The coolness of the night wrapped itself around her, encouraging her on. Tree branches lashed at her as she went, while leaves and twigs snapped under her feet. There was no trail to follow as she made her way aimlessly through the silence of the night.

After what felt like hours of running, fatigue set in, and Sally wondered if she was going in circles. She slowed her pace as she began to realize she was lost. Turning abruptly at a sound behind her, a log clipped her calf just above the ankle, throwing her to the ground. Singed by pain she wanted to cry out but another noise behind the trees stopped her. She froze. Looking up wide-eyed, a white-tailed deer stood staring at her before running away.

Trying to stand was no use. Pain gripped her every time she tried. Using her good arm and leg, she scooched herself back to where she could lean against a rock. She closed her eyes to rest, opening them only moments later, scared by the hoot of an owl overhead.

She knew she had to keep going. *When the men realize I'm gone they'll come out here looking for me. They could be out here now.* Frantic, she felt around in the darkness for a stick or branch she could use to make a splint or crutch. She found nothing.

Defeated, weak, and shivering, her silent cries gave way to a weight of exhaustion she couldn't overcome, and she slept.

FIFTEEN

At home, Finn lay back on his bed exhausted from all that had transpired. He finally fell asleep to the sounds of Goldie whining as she curled up next to him. Waking early, he dressed and grabbing his keys, snuck out of the house without waking either Mike or the dog. Getting in his Jeep and heading down the driveway, he was relieved to see the reporters, that the police had kept at bay, had finally left. The police had gone too. Relishing the cool air, he drove on until the sun rose.

Making his way towards the other side of town, he passed the roller rink where he and Sally used to go for Friday night dates. *I tried to impress her by spinning in circles around her, and then fell and sprained my ankle.* The memory made him laugh. Soon he passed the drive-in movie theater and remembered their first official date. Finally, Finn pulled in by the lot for Pine River Pond where he'd proposed to Sally. *That day had been so perfect.* His eyes began to water and his whole body felt weak. He was lost without her. Driving on, he knew he needed to refocus his thoughts and a new resolve took over. *You're out there and I'm going to find you.*

Jen arrived at the house with warm raspberry-filled croissants for the men and homemade biscuits for the dog. Mike greeted her with a warm smile.

"Mm... those smell great. I heard Finn go out early this morning," Mike said as he measured coffee into the pot. "I don't know where he went off to, but I figure he needs some space. This whole thing has been rough on him. I guess the police grilled him pretty hard."

Goldie moped down the hall towards the kitchen. "Oh, poor dog," Jen said, nuzzling the pet. "I bet you know something's up, don't you."

"Pets usually do," Mike said giving the dog one of her treats. "Let's eat and then take her for a walk. I'll let her out now, though. I don't think she was up when Finn left earlier."

Goldie barked with excitement as Mike opened the door. "Come right back, girl. You've got to have your breakfast too," he said letting her out. He watched in awe as Goldie bolted across the fields.

"She's a beautiful animal," he remarked, closing the door.

"She is and she'll be alright as soon as Sally's back," Jen persuaded. "Let's eat."

By the time they finished clearing away the dishes, thirty minutes had passed.

"I'm getting worried," Mike said. "Goldie's not back. She's never gone this long. We better go look for her." Grabbing sweaters, they headed out towards the fields calling for the dog.

"You're right. Now I'm getting scared," Jen said. "She's never taken off like this before. Can you imagine, Sally's gone and now we lost the dog! How do we tell that to Finn when he gets back?"

"Let's not panic," Mike assured. "We'll find her. She prob-

THE SKETCH

ably chased a rabbit into one of the sheds or the barn. Let's check the buildings."

After nearly an hour of searching the forty acres, Mike wasn't ready to give up. "Let's check in with the neighbors. Maybe they saw her."

Walking down the hill from the property and heading to the next, they scanned the area like hawks. Wildflowers and tall grasses bent with the breeze and the trees beyond the fields swayed. Rabbits and squirrels played games racing across the dirt and pebble driveway but there was no sign of the dog. Mike thought that if there hadn't been so much to worry about, this would have been the perfect summer day.

Jen turned to Mike, "This whole area is either farm, field or forest. There's just acres and acres of protected land out this way."

"It's beautiful. I'd love to own a piece of property out here."

"Oh yeah? What would you do with it?"

"I'm not sure. My grandparents had horses. It would be cool to have a therapy center where people could ride. You know, like veterans, people dealing with grief, or people with disabilities. They need a place where they can go and be themselves without judgment, just connect with the horses. It's what I wanted to do since I was a kid but then I grew up and ended up in business school. Once I was offered a job, I guess those thoughts just fizzled away. Being here and hearing Finn talk about Nora started to make me think about it again."

"Look at all these No Trespassing signs," Jen pointed out as they approached the neighbor's lot. "What's up with that?"

"Yeah, the place looks deserted and kind of creepy."

They rang the front doorbell of the neighbor's house several times with no response. Finally, a man looking like he'd just woken up opened the door halfway.

"Sorry to disturb you, sir," Mike began. "We're from the

property next door and our dog got away from us. We're wondering if you've seen her. She's a golden retriever."

"Nope. Sorry." The man started to close the door.

"Well, do you mind if we look around your property for her? We think she may have come in this direction," Mike pleaded.

"Your dog ain't here. We don't really want anyone on the property. There's a lot of coyotes out there. You should go. If I see your dog, I'll send her on her way." The door closed firmly.

"Well, thanks," Mike said, unsure of what to do next.

"Not too friendly," Jen noted. "We better head back to Finn's and get ready to tell him when he gets home."

"Who was that at the door?" Vic asked.

"People from next door lost their dog," Nikolai answered. "Don't worry, I mostly stayed behind the door. I got rid of them."

"I hate neighbors. Let's get the girl and be done with this. Boss wants it done today. Got the picture of the sister?" Vic asked.

"Oh yeah," Nikolai responded. "It wasn't easy sneaking in to the hospital last night. I dressed up like an orderly pushing a laundry cart. Every time I went by, someone was with her. Finally, I was able to sneak a picture through the glass window. I'm keeping the scrubs for Halloween!"

"You're so stupid sometimes. You should hear yourself," Vic laughed. "But that picture you got should put a little fear in our girl and get her talking."

The two men crossed the field towards the now-empty silo. Opening the door, the men froze in disbelief.

"What the.... Where'd she go? Didn't you tie her up good?" Vic accused.

THE SKETCH

"You were there with me. You saw her tied up," Nikolai said, as he spat on the ground.

"Then how'd she get away?" Vic snarled, his face now burning red as he boiled over with frustration. "We better find her before the boss finds out and comes after us next. You take the front fields and down to the road. I'll check out the back fields. If she ain't there we'll head into the woods."

The snap of a branch startled Sally alert and she realized it was morning. She listened as she heard more rustling in the leaves. Footfalls grew louder as they came closer. Gently, she moved to cover herself with leaves. *If the men find me, I'm done for. I have to stay alive.*

Branches broke again from the other direction, and she now feared the men were closing in from two directions. She closed her eyes and held her breath. Sounds of approach climaxed with the choir cries of the coyotes now surrounding her. Numb with a new fear, she grabbed at rocks and threw them at the pack. They stood staring, their eyes aflame. Surprised by a low grizzly growl, coming from behind, their stares faltered. Looking back and forth between Sally and the approaching dog, they scattered into the woods.

Sally drew in a breath and her beloved retriever ran to her and licked her face.

"Goldie! I love you! Thank you for finding me!" Enjoying the reunion, they snuggled together under rays of sun making its way through the branches above.

"Did you hear that?" Nikolai asked looking around him.

"Bunch of coyotes," Vic said looking out beyond the field. "I'm not too keen on going in those woods."

"Let's just tell the boss we didn't get the info and it's done," Nikolai insisted.

"Yeah. That'll work until she goes strolling in to the cops and tells everything she knows including where we kept her. The boss will be after us next," Vic said, shaking his head. "We better go looking. My Glock's at the house. Let's go back, load up and head out."

"Goldie, what are we gonna do?" Sally whispered in her dog's ear. The dog lay down next to Sally's sore leg and began to lick her aching hand. Dried blood stuck to Goldie's fur as she nudged her owner. "I don't think I can get up girl. You're going to have to get help."

Sally sat back in thought and then reached up to touch the cross she wore around her neck, the one Finn had given her for her birthday years ago. Unclasping it, she wrapped it around Goldie's collar and hooked it again. *Finn will find it and follow you back. I know it. This has to work.*

"Okay girl," Sally said, pulling Goldie's face up to hers. The dog complied. "You need to go get Finn. Find Finn."

The dog's eyes brightened and her tail wagged at the sound of Finn's name.

"Find Finn. Go. Go! Find Finn," Sally commanded.

The dog turned to go, then looked back at her. "GO! Find Finn!" Sally commanded again. This time the dog obeyed, running off in the direction she had come.

Finn returned home as Mike and Jen began making lunch.

"Hey, buddy. You hungry?" Mike asked, noticing the exhaustion on his friend's unshaven face.

"Yeah. I mean, not really," Finn hesitated, flopping into one of the kitchen chairs. "I guess I need to eat. I'm just so tired. I've been driving everywhere trying to think of where to look for Sally."

"Look Finn, there's something we need to tell you," Mike began. "We let Goldie out this morning and she hasn't come back."

"Did you look for her out by the barn? She chases rabbits out there a lot."

"Yeah, we looked everywhere. We even went over to your neighbors."

"I bet that didn't get you anywhere. Those people are so weird. I don't know what's up with them. Look, Goldie knows her way around, she'll find her way home. After I eat something and shower, I'm going to go down to the station to see if Tom knows anything more. Then I'm going to go look for Sally again."

"Sounds like a plan," Mike agreed. "We'll all go."

Sitting down to the soup and sandwiches that Jen had made, they heard scratching at the door. Finn got up to see what it was.

When he opened the door, Goldie bounded in, almost knocking him off his feet.

SIXTEEN

"Hey pup! Love you too!" Finn greeted the dog playfully as Goldie licked him. "Hey, what's this. You got blood on you. Did you catch a rabbit? Is that where you were?"

The dog pulled back from Finn and began to whine as she sat looking at the three friends. "What is it, girl?" Finn asked.

Jen was the first to see the flash of gold caught up in the dog's fur. "Hey, what's that… around her neck?"

Finn reached around the dog and unclasped the chain. "This is Sally's! It's the gold cross I gave her years ago. She always wears it. Goldie, did you see Sally?" Finn exclaimed, excited by what he saw. The dog barked her response.

"She must have found her. Mike, grab the backpack and throw some bottles of water in it. Jen, get the first aid kit. If Goldie has blood on her, it could belong to Sally. She might be hurt. I'll call Tom and let him know what's happening."

Finn left word with the police station and then tried Tom's cell phone. He could only leave a voicemail message. He paced the kitchen. "Tom, we're at my house. We think Goldie found Sally. We're heading out to go look. Call me when you get this."

Ending the call, Finn leashed the dog and the three friends followed where she led.

Crossing the fields behind Finn's house, Goldie tugged on her leash wanting to go faster. "It looks like she's taking us into the woods."

"There are acres and acres of forest out here that run behind many of the farms," Jen explained to Mike. "We'd never find her out here on our own."

"Well, we're gonna find her now," Mike assured as they climbed the three-rail fence leading into the untamed jungle of trees.

Sally heard noises in the woods, but fatigue and pain held her defenseless. Her body throbbed and she was sure she had a fever. She pulled her sweater closer around her and closed her eyes to rest, trying to ignore the pain. *I just have to trust. Goldie's a good dog. She'll find Finn. What if those guys already got to Nora? This is my fault. No. Don't think that way. Please, Finn, hurry. Help me!*

Exhaustion was pulling her down into a deep hole. *You're in shock. Stay awake.* Despite her pleas to hang on, her head fell as she slumped to the side, no longer aware of her surroundings.

The three friends kept up with Goldie's pace.

"What's back here, Finn?" Mike asked. "Like where do these woods go? What's on the other side?"

"I'm not sure. I've never hiked all the way through. It's miles and miles. She's taking us south. I think if I remember right, the river wraps around and cuts through. At the other side would be the trails behind the high school. And then beyond that of course, town. I should have grabbed a map."

"What about GPS on the phones?" Mike asked.

"No cell service," Jen replied a little out of breath, returning her phone to her back pocket.

The three stopped short pulling Goldie back at the sound of breaking branches.

"We better stay quiet," Finn cautioned in a whisper. "We don't know who's out here or what we're going to find."

"I heard something," Vic said looking over at Nikolai. He gestured that they split up by pointing to the left while he turned to the right. "It could be her. Let's go."

Spotting something up ahead, Nikolai fired his first shot.

At the explosion, wings fluttered overhead as birds scattered. A deer ran out from behind a tree, looked at Nikolai and then ran deeper into the woods. "Dang!" he mumbled under his breath.

"What'd you do that for?" Vic asked in a low voice coming back around to join his friend.

"I saw something move and thought it was her," Nikolai defended.

"Be careful next time, would ya? You almost got me."

Goldie was startled by the shot but didn't bark. Finn pulled her close and whispered approval. "Good girl!"

They moved forward now with more caution, avoiding sticks underfoot where they could. Rounding a web of tree roots, Mike silently pointed to blood he saw on the ground. Goldie urged them on. Another shot fired from behind as they increased their pace.

Deeper in the woods, Goldie knew where she was headed. After what seemed like miles of running, she pulled away from Finn, the leash slipping through his hand, and went ahead. The three friends raced to keep up with her. Finally, Goldie stopped. Sally lay slumped against a rock, pale and passed out. The dog licked her face.

"Sally!" Finn whispered excitedly. "Wake up. Wake up!"

Sally moaned.

"We have to get her to a hospital" Finn whispered to his friends. "Her hand is bloody. Give me the first aid kit." Finn proceeded to unwrap the bloody hood that dressed Sally's hand. "It's infected. Give me some gauze."

"We don't know what's wrong with her. Should we move her?" Jen asked.

"We have no choice.," Finn said as he wrapped Sally's hand. "She's probably in shock. From the way her leg is sprawled, it looks like it could be fractured, too. Mike, take Goldie's leash. I'll carry Sally."

Finn lifted her, being careful not to cause more pain. Nodding to Mike, he said, "Okay boy scout. Get your compass out. They're behind us. We can't go back that way. We have to keep going south."

Mike led with Goldie as they made their way single file through the thickest part of the woods, only resting when they got to the river.

―――

"Hey, looky here. What's this?" Vic gestured to Nikolai.

"Looks like a bloody hood, maybe the one we had on the

girl." Vic picked it up to examine it. "That means we're close. And she's hurt. She can't get far."

A coyote pack cried out, apparently still on the hunt for food.

"Maybe we should head back. I don't like them things. Their cry is creepin' me out. Besides if we're not here they'll make her their lunch instead of us," Nikolai voiced his fear.

"Too late," Vic said, gesturing for his friend to turn around. The pack of coyote circled them on all sides. "Shoot and we'll either get us some or scare 'em off."

Four shots rang out.

Two coyotes were hit and struggled to run off, crying. The others vanished.

"Did you hear that? Let's hope the coyotes got our guys," Finn said. "We need to keep going."

The sun was lower in the sky as the friends stopped to take a second break. Sipping on the last of the water they brought, Finn observed, "We haven't heard anyone or any gun shots for a while so we might be in the clear, but we need to get out of here before dark. Anybody got cell service yet?"

"Nope!" said Mike and Jen together while checking their phones.

Back at the police station, Tom tried Finn's number for the fourth time. "Pick up. Pick up."

"So, he left a message that the dog may have found Sally. Where would the dog have gone to do that?" Michelle Jacobs wondered out loud.

"Anywhere. Could be they were out for a walk at the park, or on a trail," Tom answered. "If I hadn't been in a meeting, I would have gotten the messages he left. Dang it! Why didn't the front desk patch him through to me? Now who knows what's happening?"

"Any particular parks or trails they use?" she pressed on.

"Well, Sally liked to run on the trail behind the high school. That's where she found the boy that died," Tom answered.

"Let's start there. Get a patrol car out that way."

"The trees are thinning," Mike noted. "I think we're almost out of this."

Finn agreed. "Check for cell service again."

"Got it!" Jen called out. "I'll try Tom's number."

She heard his phone ring three times and go to voice mail.

"Tom, it's Jen. We're in the woods behind Finn's, headed south. We think we're coming to the other side, near the trails behind the high school. We have Sally. She needs an ambulance."

Tom hung up from one call and saw that Jen had left a message. His heart beat faster as he anticipated her message.

"Get an ambulance out to the trails behind the high school," Tom shouted to the open room of cops. "Make it fast. We think we found our girl."

Michelle closed her laptop, grabbed her jacket, and followed Tom out.

Sixty minutes later, the EMT's had Sally hooked up to IVs inside the ambulance, Finn at her side. As they pulled away, sirens blaring towards the hospital, Tom fed Goldie treats he kept in his Bronco for happy occasions – and this was sure one.

SEVENTEEN

Tom drove Mike, Jen, and Goldie to Finn's house before going on to the hospital to check on Sally. He couldn't believe the story they were telling him about how they found her.

"The dog knew just where she was? That's so amazing. And she came back to get Finn. Wow. That's just incredible. But now there are a lot of unanswered questions that only Sally can answer, I guess," he remarked.

"Yeah, like where they had her before the woods, if they had her someplace else, and who did it, and what did they do to her?" Jen added, exhaustion seeping in.

"We'll get those answers soon," he hoped. "Listen, I can't thank you guys enough for all that you did. I'd never ask you to take that risk but I'm sort of glad you did."

"Just did what seemed right at the time," Mike said, looking at Jen, who smiled. Turning back to the chief he added, "I have to head back to Des Moines for work, but I'll be returning soon. I promised Finn I'd work on what he needs for the town's approval for his property rezoning and renovation. In the meantime, you have my number if there's anything else I can do to help."

"Much appreciated, man. Take it easy." Tom pulled away after saying his goodbyes.

"So, you'll be back?" Jen asked trying not to look eager.

"Oh, yeah. I hope we can see each other when I do." Mike's green eyes glimmered. He knew he shouldn't even ask. Finn was right. A long-distance relationship would be no good but when he looked at Jen, he couldn't stop himself from thinking about her in his future.

"Looking forward to it!" With a smile and a wave, she got in her car, leaving him with the dog.

"C'mon girl," he said leading Goldie into the house. "You deserve a thick juicy steak cooked on the grill, and a good nap."

At the hospital, Tom pushed his way through the growing number of reporters who'd come in from the larger surrounding towns and gathered since word of the boy's death, the fire, and now the kidnapping of Sally all appeared to be related. Word spread quickly when she was found.

"What happened to her?" they shouted. "Where was she? Did you find who took her?"

"No comment," Tom said, pushing their microphones away from his face.

Inside, Tom made his way to the emergency room where Finn was sitting with the Andersens. "This is an all too familiar sight. How is she?"

"Here comes the doctor now." Finn gestured towards Dr. Turley.

"I've got her leg reset. It's a minor fracture and she'll be off it for a little while. She'll need to wear a boot. The infection from the wound on her hand is bad. She's on IV fluids and antibiotics. She's weak and dehydrated and we're sedating her, so she'll be asleep the rest of the night."

"How long will she be here?" Mrs. Anderson asked.

"I'd say a couple days. She's suffering from exhaustion, and we need to assess her mental health. This has all been very traumatic. You should all go home and get some rest."

"I need to see her right away and ask her some questions," Tom insisted.

"That's not happening. At least not tonight."

"But Doc, we need to get the guys who kidnapped her. Every minute counts. There are miles of woods to search in every direction from where Finn found her. Without her help, it will be like looking for a needle in a haystack," Tom pleaded.

"I understand. Really, I do. But my patient's health comes first. I'll check on her myself tomorrow morning and give you a full update. Then we can talk about you getting to ask her your questions." The double doors swung closed as the doctor disappeared behind them.

Sally's parents decided to head for home. They hadn't been out running through the woods all day, but they were just as tired from the waiting and wondering.

"Well, Finn. I guess that leaves me to drive you home," Tom offered. "You need to eat and get some rest yourself. Mike's headed back to Des Moines and Jen went home, so it will be just you and your hero dog. Tomorrow, at first light, our officers will begin searching the woods starting behind your house. We'll follow the route you took and go from there. We're going to get whoever did this. Don't worry."

"Thanks Tom, but is Sally safe here? I don't want to leave her again. What if they come back for her?"

"There'll be a police presence at the hospital all night and they'll stay with her until we catch whoever abducted her. She'll be fine," Tom assured him as they left the hospital and headed home.

Getting into Tom's car, Finn noticed a missed call with a voicemail.

"Hey Finn, this is John Casey. Listen I found a great property for you to open your event venue, on the other side of town, and it has a cute little farmhouse on the property. With what you're being offered for your property you could buy this property and have money left over for all the renovations you need and still have cash left over. It'd be a win-win for everyone. Give me a call and I'll get you in to see the place."

Finn put the message in the phone's trash can and turned to Tom as his friend. "My lawyer left me a message. He really wants me to sell my place. He says he found me someplace else. Why do you think he wants this sale so bad?"

"I don't know. Is that something you're considering? It might be easier with the town at this point." Tom was trying to be encouraging.

"Maybe, but I'd love to raise my kids on my grandpa's land. You know, keep it in the family. Anyway, I can't think about it now. I've got bigger things to worry about.

"How did she get away?" Rodney blasted into the phone. "You guys are idiots. It's all over the news. She's at the hospital now. They'll probably have police protecting her. You get in there now before she talks, get rid of her, and get back to work. You're behind in distribution and the partners don't like it. Understand?"

"Yes, boss," Vic said, hanging up. Turning to Nikolai, he added, "Put on those orderly scrubs of yours again. You're heading back to the hospital."

THE SKETCH

Entering City Hospital just before the eleven-p.m. shift change, Nikolai walked past the front desk that had been momentarily left unmanned. *It's my lucky night,* he thought as he opened his leather jacket enough to show the lanyard around his neck with the fake ID he had made up. The scrubs he wore completed the picture of any staff member coming on for the night shift. Ducking into the staff lounge, he threw his coat on a hook and headed down the hall. Raising a light blue surgical mask up over his nose and mouth, he grabbed a linen cart left in the hall by the last guy.

He walked slowly, looking from bed to bed, not finding the woman. Turning the corner, he noticed at the very end, there was a room with a police officer sitting on guard. *Now how am I supposed to get past him?*

He pulled back into a janitorial closet. He'd learned that patience could sometimes be his best friend, so he decided he'd just give it a little while and watch for his opportunity. Sure enough, by two a.m., the halls were quiet and his friend in the officer's uniform was fast asleep.

Creeping down the hall past the cubicles with nurses who looked to be too busy to care about what was going on in the halls, he made his way past the cop, and entered Sally's room. She lay there, defenseless, and unaware of what was about to happen.

I almost feel sorry for you, Nikolai thought. *You're so pretty, and such a young thing. Now why couldn't I ever meet a nice girl like you? Ah well, you'll have to forgive me, darlin'. This really ain't my thing, but the boss says I gotta do it.*

Nikolai reached for the pillow that lay on the empty bed next to her. He fluffed it between his hands and then lifted it over her face. Leaning down to smother her, a noise stopped him.

"Don't move," a voice called out.

Still holding the pillow, Nikolai turned slowly towards the cop who was pointing a gun straight at him.

"I was just changing the linens. Thought the girl could use a clean pillow. This one's got blood or something on it." He proceeded to take the covering off the pillow in his hands.

The police officer steadied his gun. "No one's supposed to be in here. You'll have to leave."

"Well, I didn't know. Just doing my job. If they don't want us coming into rooms where people are sleeping, then why do they have us working the night shift?" Nikolai was stepping slowly past the cop towards the door. "Hey, ain't she the girl I seen on the news?" His eyes grew wide above his surgical mask. "Oh, that's why you don't want me in here. She's the one that got kidnapped at the festival or something and just got away. Do they know who done it?"

"I can't tell you that," the cop said, finally lowering his gun. "Now get going and don't come in this room again without permission."

"Alright. You don't have to tell me twice. I'm goin' and I won't tell anyone you were sleepin' either."

Nikolai left the laundry cart in the hall, grabbed his jacket from the staff lounge, and bolted for the front doors. Vic was going to have to do this job himself.

The next morning, Tom was true to his word. A half-dozen patrol cars pulled up in Finn's driveway. The cop who appeared to be in charge knocked on Finn's door. "Good morning. I'm

THE SKETCH

Sergeant Bicks. We have orders to search the woods behind your farm. Are you good with that?"

"Sure," Finn said. "No problem here. I don't think you'll find much of anything. We didn't come across anything that looked out of the ordinary. Just found her in the woods. There wasn't even a lot of blood except for right near where she was sitting."

"Well, we got to try. It's the only lead we got." The officers crossed the field behind the farm and spread out into the woods.

Nikolai let out a low whistle when he looked at the security cameras and saw police cars pass on the road below the house. "They look like they're headed next door."

"Makes me nervous, too," Vic said. "They're a little too close for my comfort. But I doubt they'll find anything except maybe them coyotes." He put on his Boston Red Sox baseball cap. "I'm heading to the hospital to finish the job you couldn't do."

"Room 103. It's at the end of the ER, across from the elevators." Nikolai offered up the information in apology for not getting the job done himself.

"Just keep things quiet here and keep an eye on the cameras. See if you notice anything else. Don't answer the door or do anything. Just keep things closed up tight like nobody's here. And run the powder so it's ready to press later. We got to get a shipment out tonight."

EIGHTEEN

Police cars came and went from Finn's property as they continued to search the woods. He wanted to stay in case they found anything, but he was anxious to head to the hospital for the morning's doctor's report. He assumed Tom would be showing up there sooner or later also. He wanted to hear everything Sally had to say to him about her abduction.

"Thought you might sleep in," Tom said, handing him a coffee as he entered the waiting area.

"I couldn't. Your Sargent Bicks showed up with his crew to search the woods before the sun was up. What time did you get here? You look like you never slept." Finn eyed the chief's rumpled uniform.

"Never did get home. Got a call about another fentanyl overdose up at the college. After I checked things out there and met the medical examiner on site, I came back here to talk with the family. We still have cops here, and on the scene, investigating. That college kid worked at this hospital part time so they're checking things out. Another young person that didn't make it.

Such a waste. Now I'm waiting to talk to Dr. Turley and see how our Sally's doing."

Vic entered the hospital by a back door under a sign that read "Receiving" and found just what he was looking for. He grabbed a package of new surgical gowns, caps, and masks. He dressed himself and scoped out the halls of the emergency room, only momentarily discouraged to find more police than expected. In minutes, he'd thought of his diversion.

Multiple blasts startled everyone – the sound of the fire alarm was deafening. From behind a cubicle curtain, Vic yelled, "Clear the building!" and chaos erupted.

An authoritative, prerecorded voice came over the loudspeaker instructing the evacuation. "Please leave by the nearest exit. Please leave by the nearest exit."

Nurses began escorting patients and visitors from the emergency room area. The investigating police officers on site, along with Tom, sprang into action to assist the people who were now going in all directions.

Vic made his way to the patient rooms at the far end and found the one that Nikolai had described. The wall sign for Room 103 hung over the door. Grabbing an empty wheelchair, he fit right in with the others who were moving patients out. Opening the door, he saw the girl lying on her side, facing away from him. He grabbed a pillow, covered the end of his silencer, and shot the brunette in the back of the head. He left the blood-soaked pillow beside her.

Exiting the room, he passed the wheelchair on to an orderly. "This room's been cleared. Check the next one," he insisted.

Throwing his surgical gown in the trash, Vic made his way to the parking lot and left. Fire engines had arrived and the fire fighters were making their way through the crowd of people and medical equipment that lined the sidewalk. Thirty minutes later, they gave the "all clear" to reenter the building.

"If there was no fire, then what was that about?" Finn asked, catching up to Tom outside the ER doors.

"I'm not sure, but I don't like it." Tom's frustration was coming through.

"Chief Dixon," Tom called out to the fire chief. "What happened?" His two-way radio clicked.

"False alarm. We've located where it was pulled and we've reset it. We're going to go through the hospital and check every floor again, just to make sure nothing else is amiss. I'll call you later with anything we find."

"Roger that."

Immediately Tom's radio crackled again. "Chief, I need back up for a possible 10-35."

"What's your location?" Tom commanded.

"First floor, far end. Room 103."

"That's Sally's room!" Finn called, following Tom into the building.

"Wait here," Tom scolded. "I need to check it out."

Finn stopped short a few feet from the room, watching the door close. Twenty minutes later, a doctor came out, followed by a nurse, Tom, and another officer.

Tom instructed the other officer with him. "Get the medical examiner here now. And I want this entire area taped off. Seal off the hospital and set up a perimeter around the parking lot. No one goes in or out." Turning to his radio, he called for any available backup.

Tom looked at Finn, who was staring wide-eyed back at him. "The nurse found her. Poor girl's been shot in the back of the head. It's not Sally."

The relief on Finn's face was clear. "Where is she, then?"

"I'm not sure. Apparently, they moved her early this morning. They had to make room for a critical patient. I'll find out who's on detail and track them down. This is good, Finn. It means Sally's safe."

"But not the girl who was lying in the bed where Sally was supposed to be. They were after her. We have to find her and make sure she's safe." Anguish filled his voice.

Dr. Turley came out of the elevator across from where Tom and Finn stood. "I just checked on our girl. You can visit her but only for a few minutes. She needs rest. We moved her up to the third floor. Your officer is up there outside the room. Excuse me now. Things have gone crazy down here. And now a helpless patient lying in her bed has been shot? The whole world is going nuts."

Sally was sitting up in bed sipping water the nurse had left her. Her face brightened when she saw Finn walk through the door. She reached out her arms, receiving his embrace.

"Oh, my love. Are you okay? I've been so worried about you." He kissed her.

"I'm okay now and so happy to see you." They kissed again until Tom cleared his throat behind them.

"I don't want to break up your reunion, but I have some questions to ask," Tom interjected.

"I don't remember much about them taking me. Just that I was headed to the shed at the festival, and I was going to call Finn but couldn't find my phone. I probably dropped it climbing the bleachers. Then I went to see if the shed was locked and the next thing I knew everything went dark. When I woke up, my hands and ankles were tied and they'd gagged me. They had a hood over my head, so I couldn't see anything." Sally became breathless telling the story.

"They said they wanted my phone. I don't know why. I think it had something to do with what I found on my computer. I heard them talking and saying something about linking things on the web. I don't know. That part's all confusing to me. After they left me, I tried to escape. It felt like I ran for hours and then I tripped on a log and I guess that's when Goldie eventually found me. I don't remember anything after I sent her to go find Finn."

"It was smart of you to put your chain on the dog so Finn would recognize it. You've remembered a lot and that's great. Take your time now," Tom cautioned her. He could see she had started to shake remembering what had happened. Finn got an extra blanket and put it around her shoulders.

Once Sally had settled back, Tom continued. "Can you remember anything about the men? What they looked like? What they sounded like? Any details about where they took you?"

"I was in a silo. I remember the smell of the rotting silage. It was awful. As for how I got out, I climbed the rails from the inside and then climbed down the chute."

"That's almost impossible," Finn gaped.

"Yeah. You didn't know I'm secretly a comic book superhero scaling silos all over town." Sally laughed with her friends, breaking the tension in the room they all felt.

"Anyway, I cut my hand on something sharp and used it to cut the bindings on my wrists. That's how I got free. I never saw the men. One had a low quiet voice. He was the nicer of the two. The other seemed older somehow. I'm not sure." Sally put her head back against the pillows to rest.

"Is that enough for now, Tom?" Finn asked, concerned.

"Yes. We'll keep a police officer outside the room, Sally, so you'll be safe. Rest up. I may have more questions for you later. Finn, can I see you outside for a minute?"

Finn followed the chief out. "Listen, I want to keep the fact that Sally is safe, quiet. If whoever killed the woman downstairs thinks they got Sally, it will keep them from coming back here and striking again. I want to use this to our advantage. Do you understand? I'll explain it to her parents, and I'll notify Dr. Turley."

"Sure. But I have to tell Jen and Mike. They'll be worried and upset. They have to know." Finn pressed.

"I don't like it, but I understand. Be careful. Call them from here where it's safest. Remember these people seem to have ears everywhere. And they might be watching you."

"Good evening! This is Laura Bristol of KGRK news. We're here standing in front of City Hospital where there was chaos earlier today. The fire department was called to this site for what turned out to be a false alarm. The police tell us that shortly after fire crews on the scene investigated, a young woman, a patient, was found shot in the head in her hospital bed. Several police were already on the scene investigating a fentanyl overdose that happened at the college overnight. The young man who overdosed, apparently worked here part time which brought the police here to ask questions. We're told tonight they were taken off that case and immediately told to search the premises for the active shooter on the loose. The hospital remains in lockdown tonight with ambulances being rerouted to other area facilities.

"Now, yesterday, we reported from here that the young woman, Sally Andersen, who had gone missing sometime during the festival, had escaped her abductors and was brought here for treatment. What we're wondering tonight is if these incidents are all tied together in some way. Police are not yet releasing the identity of the woman who was shot today inside this hospital, we assume pending notification of next of kin. But they are telling us that investigations of all the incidents are underway. Reporting live tonight, I'm Laura Bristol, KGRK news. Back to you Charlie, in the studio."

NINETEEN

"I want every silo in a ten-mile radius of Finn Webster's place checked for blood or any signs of the kidnapping." The chief's wide stance and hands on his hips commanded his officer's attention. "Focus on the farms that abut the woods. If you don't find anything there, expand the search to fifteen miles, and then twenty if needed. We'll get a search warrant if we need it, but most of these farmers won't care. Now let's get on it. Report back when you've found something."

Sally was glad to be at the hospital after her ordeal but couldn't wait to get home and start working on plans to rebuild the bakery. She needed something positive to focus on. Knowing that Tom and the entire police force were following up on her case brought some comfort, but after less than 24 hours, the stark white walls and the medicinal smell of her room became confining. She jumped at the sound of every closing door, and the beep of passing medical equipment in the hallway unraveled her. Wary of anyone who entered her room, with medicine or food, she had called, more than once, for Officer Temple stationed outside her room. Her jittery behavior did not go unnoticed by the medical team, who made frequent checks on her.

Hearing a knock at the door, she looked up to see a new face. A young woman about her age, with cropped blond hair and wearing a lab coat over a sweater and jeans peeked into the room. Seeing the woman's Nike trainers, Sally felt some instant camaraderie.

"I'm Meg Bowers. Mind if I visit for a few minutes?" she asked in a gentle, calming voice.

"Okay," Sally answered tentatively.

"I'm the therapist working with your sister, Nora, and I was wondering if we could chat a little about everything that's been going on with you both. It might help me help her."

"Sure!" Sally now sat up brightly, happy to do anything for her sister. "How is Nora? I haven't gotten to see her since she woke up. Everything happened so fast. I heard she was making progress. I was going to visit with her the day after the festival and then, well, you probably heard what happened." She looked down at her hands trembling in her lap.

"I did, but I'd like to hear it from you. Talking about it might help you feel a little less stressed. And the fire happened to both you and Nora. I want to know what you think happened. Communicating with her has been difficult. We've mostly been working through her drawings, and there are some I just can't make sense of."

Sally felt more relaxed the more she talked with Meg. Sharing her worries, concerns, and her sadness about the deaths of Jimmy, Joe, and the young woman in the hospital she didn't even know, released a burden she'd been carrying. It felt good to share more than just the details that the police kept quizzing her on.

The therapist listened intently as Sally shared what she remembered of the fire and all that had happened to her, asking only a few prodding questions and offering words of comfort when needed. When Sally seemed worn out from the emotional retelling, she sat back thoughtfully before offering her idea for a next step.

"Dr. Turley and I have been talking and we were wondering how you felt about going up to visit Nora while you're here. And I'd like to spend some time with you and your sister together. Maybe you'd be willing to share a room with her? I bet Nora would love that. We're thinking just a night or two and then maybe you can both be discharged together. How does that sound?"

Sally's face lit up in contrast to her eyes, now red rimmed from the tears she had wept during her telling of her story to the therapist. "I'd love that. Oh, thank you."

Within the hour, Sally was being wheeled into Nora's room.

"Sally! Sally!" Nora's smile matched the brightness in her eyes. Seeing her sister made her cry what they referred to as her happy tears.

"Hey sis! Looks like you've got a new roommate!" Sally reached from her chair wrapping as much of her body alongside her sister in a hug as she could manage, without crushing her injured leg or her hands which bore the bruises of her escape.

Nora giggled and clapped, her love for her sister evident.

Meg followed into the room behind Sally. "Officer Temple is right outside, so you'll both be very safe. Nora, I wondered if you could show Sally some of the sketches you've been drawing for me."

Nora already had her sketch pad in hand and was drawing a picture of Sally in her wheelchair.

"Great, Nora! Now my hospital visit will be remembered forever." The three women laughed.

Meg spent the entire afternoon helping Nora and Sally work through the events of the fire. She'd agreed with Sally beforehand not to mention the kidnapping, feeling that it would be too much for Nora to understand. But she'd offered to talk more with Sally separately about it, anytime she wanted or needed to.

As Sally flipped through Nora's sketch book, she came across a few pictures of people she didn't recognize.

"It's not unusual to find portraits of people we don't know," Sally began. "Nora sketches everyone and everything that catches her eye. I always thought of it as her way of remembering and also communicating about how she saw things from her perspective. Like this picture." Sally held up a sketch. "This is the delivery guy at the back door of our bakery. Nora, I'm guessing you're trying to tell me here that the guy wasn't late but instead stopped to have a smoke and text on his phone."

Nora smiled, and rocked back and forth in her bed as she clapped.

Sally continued, "Most of Nora's pictures tell a story but some of her pics are just random. Like this one." Sally held up a picture of a young boy in the street feeding an ice cream cone to his dog. "Obviously the moment touched her. She has a way of seeing things that you or I wouldn't even take notice of. It's a beautiful gift.

"Here's another one. Hmmm, this is strange." Sally held up a picture of a man wearing a Red Sox baseball cap. "I think I saw this guy before. He came in to the bakery just after Jimmy Dalton died. I remember because of the baseball cap. I'm pretty sure it's the same guy. You don't see too many Red Sox fans in these parts. Nora, when did you see this guy? You weren't there that day. I can't tell from the picture when it was done."

Nora looked at the picture, glanced away and stared quietly

out the window opposite them. Meg sat forward on her seat noticing the change in Nora's reaction.

"Are there any more of this man in that book?" Meg urged Sally to continue looking.

"Just one, from what I see. Looks like the same man sitting in a van," Sally pointed out.

Nora remained quiet and eventually laid back against her pillows and shut her eyes.

"Let's leave it there for today," Meg suggested. "I bet both you guys are tired. I'll let you rest. We'll talk more tomorrow."

Wanting to give Nora a break after the marathon therapy session, Sally made her way to her own bed. A knock on the door brought both women alert with renewed energy as Finn entered bearing gifts of milkshakes for all.

"Oh Finn, you and your milkshakes are the best medicine," Sally gushed, reaching out for a hug.

"I heard you two were going to be roommates. Nora, I hope you still like peppermint flavored, 'cause that's what I got you."

Nora nodded her head repeatedly, eyes wide like saucers, reaching out to take her drink from his hands.

"Remember back in high school when I tried to make them for us and I didn't have the lid of the blender on right?" Finn sighed, leaning back in the chair he'd taken. "What a mess that was! We had it in our hair and I had to explain to my mom why there was chocolate on her kitchen curtains. She was so mad at first but then cracked up laughing at us."

The three friends were laughing easily together when Finn's phone rang. Mike's name came up on the caller ID.

"Hey Mike, I'm here with my two favorite girls. How are you?"

"Not bad. Hey, I don't want to interrupt all the fun it sounds like you're having but I've got some news for you."

"Is this about the renovations for our property?"

"Yeah. I've been digging in to the owners of the land surrounding you in an effort to appeal to them. Getting their agreement would sure save a lot of time instead of having to do a traffic study of similar properties and all the other things the town wants you to do.

"All the land behind you is state preservation land, so none of that is a concern. On one side of you there's a property that was a farm that's been rezoned for business. You don't see much because of the trees that line that side of your property, but it looks like some kind of small distribution warehouse has gone up there. Small trucks and vans keep going in and out of the property."

"Really?" Finn was surprised. "I guess I haven't been that observant. I've been so busy since I got back. I think I did hear the family that owned that farm moved away. Find anything else?"

"It's not clear to me what they're distributing. But a business can't object to what you want to do. Now listen to this. Just for the heck of it, I looked up the tax records of when that was rezoned and who purchased it. It's the same company that bought up the farm on the other side of you. You know, that crazy rude neighbor of yours. And get this, your lawyer, John Casey brokered both deals."

Back at the police station, Tom took calls from his officers who'd spent the morning searching the silos. He gritted his teeth and rubbed the back of his neck in frustration as each one reported they'd found nothing.

Doug Briggs quietly entered the chief's office and set himself down at the small conference table covered with papers. Moving the case files that lay there in what looked like no particular order, he set down two roast beef sandwiches oozing with sauce. The whiteboard looming across from him with pictures of the fire, Jimmy Dalton's body in the creek, and the dead girl with the bullet wound in her skull, did nothing to deter his appetite.

"Are you sharing those or is that a serving for one?" Tom asked, dropping a pile of napkins on the table.

"Help yourself. There's more where I got these," Doug offered. "No luck searching the silos?" he asked, already guessing at the answer.

"No. If Sally says it was a silo, then she was kept in a silo. I just don't get it. What are we missing?" Tom asked more to himself than to the agent across from him.

"You're from this farming town, not me, but I understand there's been a lot of transition in this area. So, if all the silos were checked and they were all full, she obviously couldn't have been there. Did your guys check all the farms? Even the ones that aren't farms anymore? Don't some of them still have silos on their properties?"

"I told them to check ALL the silos. I'll have Bicks go down the list again and mark off all those no longer farming, and we'll check them again. Any luck with her phone?"

"Forensics is still working on it. We were able to download her iCloud account and go back into the deleted history. You know the history never really goes away, right? Anyway, we got to see the host pages the Jimmy Dalton boy was looking at. On the surface they're all dead ends – fake web pages. But they all lead back to somewhere into the dark web. These guys use encryption code to hide. Some of it's good and some of it's very good. But once in a while, we get lucky and some of it's poorly done, and we get in. Sometimes we find similarities to code in other cases. The more people use the internet and social media to find prescription drugs, those opportunities are increasing every day. We have our best people working on it.

"Look," he continued, "I know you want to know who did all these crimes in your town. I get that, but I want to take down the big boss, the guy at the top who controls the strings. I want to put him, whoever he is, and all his buddies, away before more lives are destroyed."

TWENTY

Finn had trouble concentrating on his work the next morning. His focus on the financial reports in front of him was repeatedly interrupted by lingering curiosity about his neighbors. Needing to take some action, he went outside with his camera drone and remotely lifted it above the trees that bordered his property to see what he could see.

The news from Mike about who owned the property on both sides of him, was troubling. He couldn't place his finger on why. He snapped a few pictures feeling only slightly guilty that what he was doing could be misconstrued as spying.

The pictures he took, one of the empty warehouse with only a couple cargo vans parked on the lot, and the other of the neighbors farmhouse with a back yard littered with trash, didn't tell him much. Still, he thought having something to look at might trigger the answers he was looking for.

I need to go see John Casey after I visit with Sally and Nora at the hospital this afternoon. He'll have to tell me something. I need to put this gnawing in my gut to rest.

About mid-day, Goldie was in the kitchen enjoying a cool

breeze through the open screen door when a brown delivery van pulled up. One bark from the dog alerted Finn to greet the driver and receive his package. Tearing open the brown paper box, he turned to the dog, "This is for you, girl. How about I put this on you, and we go show our friends at the hospital?" Goldie wagged her tail in delight as Finn placed the new trinket around the dog's neck.

One call to clear the visit with Dr. Turley and they were on their way. The drive through the shady back roads of Glen Rock was uneventful except for the retriever who enjoyed every minute with her head out the window, ears and jowls flapping in the wind, tongue hanging out to the side.

Entering the main doors of the hospital, the receptionist, already alerted by Dr Turley of the dog's visit, had a special "visitor" sign attached to a shortened lanyard ready to put around Goldie's neck. Meg, also there waiting, escorted Finn and the dog to the women's shared room.

"So, how are they doing?" Finn asked as they walked.

"Pretty well. We're looking at a discharge in the next day or two. I think both women will feel better when they're home and, we've probably done as much as we can for them. I'm glad you're here. From what I've heard, Nora seems to open up to you and there's something that still seems to be troubling her. I'm not sure if she's trying to remember something or she's forcing herself to forget. If we can get at it today, then I'd feel good about sending her home."

Entering the room, Goldie nearly tipped over the tray table that stood next to Nora's bed. Her excitement over seeing both sisters had her bouncing back and forth between the beds, clearly eager for the pets and hugs the women offered.

THE SKETCH

"Oh, Finn!" gushed Sally. "You good man. Thank you for bringing her! Hey, what's this around her neck?"

Sally held the dog close and pulled from the fur of her scruff a gold chain with a heart shaped charm inscribed with the words "Hero Dog".

"That's great! I love it! And, she deserves it." They all laughed easily, enjoying the dog's visit.

Noticing that Nora was quick to pick up her sketch pad and begin drawing, Meg moved in closer to her bed to watch. She was amazed by Nora's skill as the first strokes began to take the shape of Finn and the dog.

"Nora, your skill for drawing is really something," Meg began. "Can we look at some of your other sketches in your book? I'm sure there are some that Finn hasn't seen yet." Nora handed her the book.

"Finn, yesterday we were looking at some pictures here and Sally noticed a few with people she didn't know. One person may have looked familiar to her. Whoever the person was, talking about the picture made Nora feel uncomfortable. Would you mind taking a look and see if it's a picture of someone you recognize?"

"Here," Sally offered, reaching for the book to leaf through the pictures. "I'll find it for you. It's a guy wearing a Red Sox baseball cap."

"A Red Sox fan?" Finn questioned. "You don't see many of those around here. I'd remember someone like that, so, sure, I'll take a look."

Taking the book Sally handed him, Finn gazed at the picture, his face becoming serious and drawn of all emotion.

"What is it?" Meg asked.

It took Finn a moment to respond. "I think I know this guy."

He looked over at Nora and then back at the picture. Stepping closer to the bed he slowly turned it to show her. Goldie inched closer to Nora's bed, and sensing that something troubled the woman, rested her head on the edge. Nora stretched out her arm and gently curled her fingers in the dog's fur.

"Nora, where did you see this man?" Finn asked in a soft gentle voice.

Nora began stroking the dog's head. "B..b..b..ba." Nora struggled to get the words out.

"Take your time, sweetie," Sally encouraged as she reached to hold Nora's other hand.

Nora tried again, "B..b..b..bake."

"You saw him at the bakery?" Sally asked.

Nora nodded.

"Finn, how do you know him?" Sally asked, now looking at the picture again.

"He's my neighbor." Finn took the book and began looking at more of the sketches.

"Okay, well that makes sense," Sally said thinking out loud. "I think I remember seeing him at the bakery not long after Jimmy Dalton died. I sort of remember him coming in with another guy, but I couldn't tell you what he looked like. I just remember the baseball cap on this one. Anyway, if he's a neighbor he probably just came in for coffee and we're bound to see him around town."

"Except," Finn interjected, "here he is again in this other sketch. It looks like he's sitting in a van."

"Nora, where did you see this man sitting in a van?" Finn asked turning to her.

Nora continued to pet the dog while staring at the wall ahead. "B..b..b." she struggled again with the words.

"He was outside the bakery?" Sally asked slowly pacing her words.

Nora nodded again.

THE SKETCH

It was Meg's turn to ask some questions. "Nora, something about this man is upsetting you. Can you tell us what it is about him that is making you feel uncomfortable?"

Nora just stared expressionless at the wall.

Sally and Finn silently locked eyes, both now wondering what Nora might be wanting to tell them.

Meg pushed on. "Can you draw us a picture, Nora, that would help us understand?"

Finn gently removed Nora's hand from the dog's head and put her pencil in it. He rested the sketch pad on her lap. Sally released the hand she was holding, and Nora began to draw.

A few minutes passed as if Nora was thinking about what to create and then without using words, she began her picture as the three watched. When Nora finally finished, she put her pencil down, closed her eyes and laid her head back on her pillow.

Finn took the sketch book and silently passed it on to Sally. Their eyes locked again. Meg reached out for the book and stared intently at the picture.

Sally prompted. "Nora, did you see this man the night of the fire?"

Nora, eyes still closed, nodded. She reached out and began to stroke the dog who had patiently waited beside her.

Finn pressed for more information. "Nora, did you see him before the fire started or later, after the fire started?"

Nora sat motionless, staring at the wall across from her, twirling around her fingers the strands of brown hair that hung just below her shoulders.

"She doesn't seem able to give us any more information today. How about I try again tomorrow?" Meg asked, hopeful they were at least starting to make some progress.

Sally nodded in understanding that they had pushed hard enough for answers. Her sister was clearly getting overwhelmed.

"So, this man was sitting in a van at the bakery sometime the night of the fire," Finn repeated to the group. "I need to take this to the police."

"How about if for now you take a picture of the sketch with your phone?" Meg suggested. "Would that be enough for now and then if they need it later, we can give it to them? I don't want to take anything from Nora right now. And, I'd like to have it when I talk to her a little more about it later. It might help her."

Finn snapped a photo of each of the sketches before offering to get them some snacks from the cafeteria. He sensed that ice cream sandwiches all around might cheer the room before taking his leave with the dog.

"Finn, we can't just bring a guy in for questioning because he's a lousy neighbor," the chief stressed after looking at printouts of the photos Finn had just shown him.

"I want to hear Finn out," Doug interjected. "We don't know for sure how anything is related yet but I wouldn't be a good DEA agent if I didn't look at every detail, no matter how insignificant it might seem at first."

The three sat around the conference table in the chief's office mulling over what they knew and trying to decide on what to do next.

"Let's go through this again," Doug prodded.

Finn began with a rough breakdown of events.

"I went to the neighbor's house to introduce myself and the guy barely opened the door enough to talk. He was, let's just say, unwelcoming. Even Goldie didn't like him. She was growling and pulling away the whole time we were there. Then Mike and Jen went over the day they couldn't find Goldie and he, or someone else that lives there, was just as rude to them. Whoever it was that answered the door wouldn't let them search for our dog. Now Nora is telling us that this guy, who's my neighbor, was at the bakery the night of the fire."

"Well, my first question - and don't take offense to this - is Nora reliable in what she's saying?" Doug asked.

"Yes. Definitely," Finn confirmed. "She might be autistic, but she is one of the smartest people I know. She has trouble communicating so if you don't know her, you might think otherwise. But I grew up with her. I know her. She can only express herself with honesty."

"Okay, fair enough. I had to put the question out there because if anything comes of this, others will be asking. Now, did Sally or anyone else say they saw this guy at the bakery that night?" Doug asked.

"No. Sally says she remembers him coming in to the bakery with another guy right after Jimmy Dalton was found but that's the only time she can think of."

"Like I said, it's not enough to bring a guy in. People are allowed to sit in their vehicles," the chief piped in. "But maybe it's enough so we could visit and ask if he saw anything that night that looked suspicious while he sat there." He looked at Doug who nodded in agreement.

"Could you send a copy of this picture to your buddy, Mike, and see if he was the guy who answered the door when he went to visit the neighbor? It might just tell us if we're talking about one person or two if anything comes of this." Doug was looking at all the angles and this encouraged Finn.

"Yes, I will," Finn agreed. "And there's something else. I don't know if it's related to all this or not, but Mike has been doing some research for me for the permits I need for the rezoning application for my land. He called yesterday to tell me that the limited liability company that bought the land west of me is the same company that owns the land that we're talking about where this neighbor is. And, according to my lawyer, John Casey, the company, at least I think it's the same one, wants to buy my land for well above normal asking price. John brokered both those deals and now apparently is trying to get me to move so he can have in on the sale of my land. I was going to go have a talk with John myself this afternoon to find out more before all this came up with Nora's sketches."

"You can't blame your lawyer for wanting a commission. What makes you think it's the same LLC that wants your land?" Doug asked.

"Because in one of my conversations with John, he mentioned it was a firm from Boston that was interested in the land. This LLC is out of Boston. Listen, he doesn't just want the sale. He's been pestering me about it. He used to be a family friend but at the last town meeting he spoke out against me and my plans for the land. The other day he called and said he found another place for me to move and was really pushing me to sell. I just don't get it. Something's up with him."

"Hmm…well that's interesting," Doug interjected. "Or it's just a coincidence. This LLC is out of Boston and your neighbor who sat outside a bakery on the night it burned down is a Boston Red Sox fan. Finn, go home. I think Tom and I should go meet this lawyer friend of yours by ourselves and see what he has to say before we go visit your neighbor. We'll catch up with you there if we learn anything new that you should know."

TWENTY-ONE

The police chief and the DEA agent walked the two blocks to the courthouse where they were certain they'd find the attorney, John Casey. Calling his office ahead, they learned he'd be there all afternoon. He was on call for a new program that lent itself to court reform. Every attorney in town was expected to pick up at least one new pro bono case a month, representing people who couldn't afford normal attorney fees. The two men thought making their visit look like a coincidence might get the lawyer to talk more openly when they approached him with their questions.

They weren't wrong. As soon as they approached the lawyer, sitting on the wooden bench in the main hallway, he got up to greet Tom like an old friend.

"This is an acquaintance of mine," Tom said, introducing Doug without giving away his purpose for being there.

After some small talk, Tom began his discreet questioning. "By the way, John, I heard you were involved in the sale of the land out by Finn's place. Any ideas what they're using it for?"

"Some sort of warehouse, I guess. I don't know too much about it."

"And, did I hear right? The same people bought up the land on the other side?" Tom pressed on.

"I don't know about that," John answered, looking back and forth between the two men.

"Well you brokered both deals, didn't you?" Tom continued.

"You know I can't talk about my clients, Tom." The lawyer shifted his feet and was clearly becoming uncomfortable.

"I was just curious if it's the same company that wants Finn's place. You know, the poor guy just wants to make something of his family's land. I noticed at the town meeting that you started the objections to the rezoning and got everyone else fired up against him," the chief added, still pressing for more information.

"I just spoke my mind." John eyed the chief. "You suggesting something?"

"Nope. Just curious. By the way, how's your wife?"

"The chemo's worse than the disease," the lawyer said, looking away from the two men toward the court room doors. "Looks like I'm needed. Thanks for the chat, gentlemen."

"He's a curious one," Doug commented as they left the building. "Think there's something going on he isn't telling us?"

"Yup! Let's go talk to Finn's neighbor."

Riding in the DEA agent's black Suburban up the gravel drive, Doug couldn't help but notice the "No Trespassing" signs posted every twenty-five feet. "Is that normal for these parts?" he asked the chief.

"Some people do it to ward off hunters but it's not common," the chief explained.

The agent strained his neck to look up at the trees.

"What are you looking at?" Tom asked, his eyes following in the same direction.

"Not what I'm looking at but what I'm looking for. Just curious if someone who wants this much privacy has any cameras hidden. Yup. There's one," he said pointing up into the trees.

The chief looked up. "No law against it, but I guess they know we're here."

Vic opened the door as the two men approached. Noting the chief's uniform, he struggled to be polite.

"Hello, gentlemen. How can I help you?"

"I'm Chief Bashill. This is Agent Briggs. We were wondering if you could answer a few questions for us."

"If I can."

"What's your name?" The chief held his small notepad ready to take notes.

"Why do you want to know?"

"Could you step outside here on the porch, sir? It might be easier to talk."

Vic stepped out on to the porch and lit a cigarette after carefully closing the door behind him.

"Now, let's try this again. What's your name, sir?"

"Vic Comenti."

"And you live here?"

"Yup."

"You own the place?"

"Nope. Renting."

"Who are you renting the place from?" the chief asked, wishing he could bring this guy to the station for questioning. There was something about him, he just didn't like.

"Can't say. I just called a number and sent the first month's payment. It's all done through autopay."

"I see." The chief made a note on his pad. "Vic, we have a witness in a case we're investigating. They said they saw you sitting in a van outside the bakery building on the night a fire took place down there on Main Street. We're wondering if you remember that night and if you saw anything suspicious while you were there."

"Can't say I remember that or seeing anything suspicious at any time. I'm new around here." Vic stared the man straight in the eye, not showing any signs of flinching at the questions he was being asked.

"Where'd you move from?"

"Up north. Now, gentlemen, I'm sorry I can't help you. I got to get back to what I was doing."

"Well, thank you. We'll be back in touch if we need anything more."

Tom and Doug got back in the Suburban and drove down the hill slowly so they could take a last look around the property.

"Think he's hiding something?" Doug asked.

"Oh yeah. Something's going on. His story about renting the place smells fishy," the chief agreed.

"Notice anything while we were there?"

"Like the place is run down and there's lots of trash at the side of the house?" Tom observed.

"And he's got a silo sitting out back there. I'd like to run this guy's name and see if he's got any priors."

The chief picked up his radio and patched into the station. "Bicks, I'm up at the farm next door to Finn's. It doesn't look like it's being farmed. Did you check the silo out here?"

"Yes sir," the officer replied, shuffling his papers, looking through his lists. "That silo was full of fresh silage, sir."

"I want you to run this guy's name, Vic Comenti, and see if he's got any priors. Then call the Weaver Grain Depot and find out when they delivered that silage up here. Then I want you to run a check on the property owner and see what you come up with. I want anything that will get me a warrant to search this place with the dogs and I want it tonight."

Turning to the DEA agent he asked, "You got plans for later?"

"I do now."

———

"The boss ain't gonna like this," Vic said, heading down to the basement.

"I don't get it. What witness saw us that night? We didn't see anyone. It can't be that girl who owned the bakery. You shot her in the hospital, and I hear her sister's coo-coo," Nikolai reasoned.

Vic looked around the basement room at all the blenders full of powder, the boxes of empty capsules, and the already full crates ready to go to the warehouse for shipping. "We better pack it up and move out."

"Wait. We got another shipment ready to go out tonight. Let's get paid first. Then go."

"Okay. I don't wanna leave my cut behind either. We'll wait until tomorrow to call the boss, and then we're out."

———

Finn waited at home through early evening, hoping the chief would call with some news. When it started to get dark and he hadn't heard anything, he began to wonder what else he could do. He sat on his front porch scanning the horizon. He had the urge to send his drone up and check on his neighbors' activities again but didn't feel comfortable with being that intrusive. It was then that the call he was waiting for came through.

Finn packed the dog for a night at the Andersens and returned home to brew a fresh pot of coffee. It was going be a long night.

The clock in the kitchen ticked past eleven p.m. as Finn heard the first tires creep up his drive. No headlights could be seen but he knew they were there. Peering through the window he saw the outlines of five police cars and four black SWAT vans pull into his lot. Without being told, the police grabbed their gear from the car trunks while the SWAT team set up a staging area. Before the DEA agent had time to pull up in his black SUV, the officers were fanning out among the trees that surrounded the properties on both side of Finn's. A knock came at the door and he knew it would be the chief reminding him to remain inside.

"You got the dog someplace safe?" the Chief asked.

"Yup."

"But you had to stay? I told you it might not be safe for you if bullets start flying. Who knows what these guys are capable of."

"Chief, I want to see this through. I put coffee on if any of your guys need some. Whatever you need, just ask."

"Thanks."

"But Tom, how did you know?"

The chief's radio crackled. "I got to go. Stay put. Never mind. I know you won't. I cleared you to hang at the staging area. You'll be able to hear what's going on. Just don't get in the way."

Thirty minutes later, Finn stood between the chief and the DEA agent, wearing a bulletproof vest an officer had handed him. A rather tall, hefty man wearing a black T Shirt with the letters S.W.A.T. on the back joined them. The newcomer wore a black knit hat that covered just the top of his head, black gloves, and all the firearms a man could possibly strap to his body.

"Ready folks?" the chief asked, turning to his colleagues. "We're on radio silence. SWAT makes the call on three."

"Got it."

A field officer ran up to the tent they were huddled under. "Chief, we got a guy loading up a van from the house."

"It's go time, gentlemen," the SWAT officer announced in a deep voice that matched his build. "On my mark...three, two, one! GO. GO. GO."

Spotlights flashed, illuminating the sky on all sides. The chief and the DEA agent along with two other police officers piled into Doug's SUV and headed for the neighbor's house.

The radio cackled. "We got a runner, Chief."

The SUV pulled up in time to see two officers bang in the front door with a battering ram. Two other officers were out in the back field tackling the man they knew as Vic. Another officer stood by the silo with a barking police dog.

"Looks like we got 'em," the chief exclaimed.

Finn, overjoyed, punched the air in silence as he continued to listen from the staging area. The two officers who had entered the house were heard on the radio. "First floor clear." After a pause the other officer added, "We need hazmat in here."

It was Doug's turn to get involved. "What are we talking about?"

"We got pills and white powder. Looks like fentanyl."

TWENTY-TWO

The police station buzzed with people, which was unusual for the middle of the night. Finn sat, savoring a long, overdue coffee with the chief and the DEA agent, who took turns filling him in on what they'd learned that afternoon that led up to their busting in to his neighbor's house next door.

"Once Nora identified your neighbor as a potential suspect in the arson fire at the bakery, we went to see him. Doug thought right away the house might've been being used as a drug den, but we weren't sure. He noticed the cameras all over the property and the 'No Trespassing' signs. All the trash along the side of the house gave them away too. They're all signs of making drugs and the paranoia that goes along with it. They hold on to trash so no one goes through it and put up the signs to keep people away. But the little detail that brought these two guys down as the ones who kidnapped Sally was the silo. No one keeps silage unless they're farming. When we checked it out, we determined that the Weaver Grain Depot made a delivery there the morning Sally escaped. These guys were so busy searching for her we figure they forgot to cancel the order once they realized she was gone. They intended to suffocate her in that silo. We're dumping it now and I'm certain we'll find the blood evidence we need confirming she was kept in there."

"What about the warehouse and the LLC that owns the two properties?" Finn asked.

"The warehouse was being used to move large amounts of product," Doug offered up. "There wasn't anyone there when we busted in but there's enough evidence of its use. We're working now to trace it all back to the LLC in Boston."

"John Casey! My lawyer. He's got to know," Finn shared, his enthusiasm for answers overtaking his exhaustion.

"Bicks picked him up earlier. He seems pretty frail. We're headed to question him now before we interrogate this guy Vic and his partner. We're going after everyone involved in this mess and we're counting on one of these guys to squeal. Head home, Finn. We'll be in touch."

Tom entered the room where John Casey waited, noticing that the man he was about to question looked old and scared instead of the prominent, confident lawyer he knew him to be. They sat in silence across the table from each other until John couldn't take it anymore.

"Your officer told me you arrested a couple of guys renting a property I sold. I don't think I can tell you anything about them."

"We know you're connected to what was going on, John. You sold that property where a lot of drugs have been going out from and you've been working to sell other properties to the same guy. Are you telling me you didn't know what they were using the properties for?"

"I'm sorry, Tom. Attorney-client privilege. I can't tell you anything. I'd be disbarred."

"Is that how you want to play it? You're being charged as an accessory, John. You think you won't be disbarred after that?"

"Accessory to what? You can't tie me to anything. I just helped sell some properties."

"John, we've known each other a long time. Don't try to fool me. You sold properties to some bad people who are making pills that get put on the streets and kill our kids. You're in deeper than you realize. Look, I know your wife's been sick and the bills were piling up. But we checked in with the hospital and you're all paid up. I'm guessing if we checked your bank account, we'd find some extra deposits there, too. Is that why you got involved with these creeps?"

John crumpled over in his chair, already exhausted by the few questions he'd been asked. "You don't understand. I was desperate. My wife is so sick and her treatments cost money - money we didn't have." Tears filled his eyes.

"Why don't you just start from the beginning and tell me what happened," Tom calmly prompted.

"This guy just came to my office one day looking for land to buy. His name is Rodney. He's from the Boston area. I don't even know his last name. His name wasn't on the business card he left. The deals all went through an LLC. He heard I'd brokered some other deals and wanted me to work for him.

"One day, we got to talking and I told him about my wife being so sick and in so much pain and I guess because he listened so nicely and I was so consumed with worry, I told him about how desperate I was for money. He said he could help me out. He said he had some pain killers that worked great for him when he had some surgery a while back and he thought they would help her. Then he said he'd pay me well if I could set him up with some properties.

"I hope you understand why I couldn't refuse. I needed the money, Tom. I thought there'd be little risk. I knew Finn's grandfather was dying and I never thought Finn would move back so it was a no brainer. I set him up with the lots that abut that property and just waited until the old man died. By then, he'd been sending me pills for my wife and she was finally comfortable. She can't go without them now - and he was paying her medical bills.

"When Finn said he was staying and not selling his family land, the guy got mad. I tried to back out of the deal, but he said I was in too deep and that I'd have to pay him back for all the pills and the hospital bills he'd been paying. He even sent his thugs to beat me up. I had no choice then. I had to get Finn to agree to sell the land. Tom, I didn't do anything illegal. I took his cash and some pills, that's all. I'm not involved in whatever they did. I just tried to get Finn to sell his land, that's all. I don't know anything about these people. I swear."

Tom was sitting back in his chair in silence, staring at the old man across from him. He felt sorry for him but knew he wouldn't be able to just let him go. He took from his file pictures of Vic and Nikolai and placed them in front of the lawyer.

"Do you know these guys?"

John looked at the pictures and then turned away. "I recognize them. One was with Rodney at the town meeting. The other guy is the one that beat me up when I tried to back out of my deal with them."

"I'm sorry you went through all this, John. You got in with the wrong people. If only you'd come to me, or anyone, when you needed help. We'd have been there for you. That's the beauty of a small town." Tom shook his head as he got up to leave. "I'll send in an officer who'll take your statement. The DA will want to talk to you and no doubt you'll be asked to testify."

Doug left the observation room and met Tom in the hallway. "That was tough to watch. You really going to charge him as an accessory?"

"That's up to the DA. He took illegal drugs and bribes but no, I doubt he'll be charged. I just had to scare him a little to get him to talk. Poor man, and such a nice guy. Are you ready to go interview the real bad guys?"

"Let's go."

Doug and Tom entered the interrogation room where Vic Comenti sat waiting impatiently.

"Remember us?" Doug asked as he removed his jacket and rolled up his sleeves.

Vic sat silent, now staring out the only window in the room.

"Guess you've been more than just renting that farmhouse as a place to live. From what we've seen you've got yourselves a nice little business going. With what we found in that basement and what we suspect we'll find in that silo, you could be looking at going away to prison for a long time. Tell us who you're working for and maybe we can make a deal?"

"I'm not saying nothin'. I want my lawyer. I get a call, don't I?"

"Are you sure about that lawyer? Seems like you've got a lot on the line here. We've got a dead boy in the woods, an arson fire, the murders of Joe from the diner and the girl in the hospital, kidnapping, and a whole lot of drugs. Tell us what we want to know and maybe we can get that death sentence off the table."

"I want to call my lawyer, John Casey. He'll get me out of here tonight."

"You might want to rethink that Vic. You see, he's sitting with an officer right now telling what he knows."

Vic hesitated, then leaned forward and looked Doug straight in the eye. "LAWYER!"

Doug and Tom left without further questions and headed down the hall to interrogate his partner Nikolai.

"Nikolai Bradcoff," Doug began. "You have an interesting choice of friends you do business with. We just heard a lot about your involvement with selling drugs to the kids in this town and the kidnapping of a certain young woman, not to mention a story about you visiting the hospital to kill a woman. Care to tell us your side of things?"

"Yeah, you didn't hear nothing. Nobody's talking to you. You're bluffing." Nikolai sat back, his wrists tugging against the chains that bound him to the table.

"You want to take that chance?" the agent challenged. "You got a lot of time in prison coming based on what we've heard – a whole lifetime in prison. You tell your side of the story and maybe things don't go so south for you."

"What'd Vic tell you? None of this was my idea. I just did what I was told."

"And what was that?" the police chief urged.

"Business was going good and then that high school kid died. It was then that things got crazy. Look, I can't talk about it. Vic will get mad and he's real nasty when he's mad."

"We know you were making pills to distribute," Doug prodded.

"Yeah, for the boss in Boston. That's where Vic and I are from. He gave Vic a job when we were in high school, and I tagged along. Worked for him ever since. It's just a job."

"What this guy's name, the one you worked for in Boston?"

"Rodney. That's what Vic calls him. I don't know anything more about him except he can get real nasty too."

"Tell us more about making the pills."

"Everything was going great and then Vic got this idea that we could start a little business on the side and sell some of the product local. He's good with computers and stuff. He did some advertising. It was all handled by computers and through the mail. Then this one local kid answered an ad and Vic went to meet him. I don't know what happened after that except Vic got worried the next day when he heard about the kid found dead and that it was from the pills he gave him. The stupid kid must have taken too many or the amount of powder we put in was off. That can happen, you know. We're not scientists. Anyway, Vic said we had to do something to make sure it didn't get traced back to us. Somehow Rodney found out – he's got eyes and ears everywhere. Next thing I know we're told to plant bugs in all the places the kid hung out at so we could hear what people were saying. We even sat behind you, Chief, in the bakery, the day we planted the bugs there."

Doug looked at Tom, who shook his head in disbelief, and then turned back to Nikolai who was on a roll.

"Continue."

"We heard that lady talking with her friends about asking questions, so we threatened them by throwing bricks through their windows, but they didn't stop."

"What did you do then?" Tom pressed on.

"That one night, we heard the lady call her boyfriend and tell him that she found the computer the kid used to buy the drugs and we knew we had to get her computer to destroy the evidence. We poisoned the dog so it'd be too sick to bark if she heard us. We were only going to torch the computer, but Vic poured stuff everywhere and the fire got out of hand real fast. Vic insisted on taking the cash from the register on the way out. We barely got out of there alive."

"Vic was with you? You both started the fire?" the chief confirmed.

"Yeah. Then after the fire we were still trying to make sure the cops couldn't get her computer history and trashed emails. Rodney told us to get the lady's iCloud account information so we could hack in and delete everything. This cloud thing keeps everything I guess."

"So that's when you kidnapped her?"

"Yup. We followed her until she was alone. But she didn't have her phone and couldn't remember her passwords. We didn't hurt her. I even brought her a sandwich and told her not to be afraid. I didn't know Vic and Rodney were planning to kill her anyway. And then she got away. Oh man, was Vic mad. He made us go into them woods and risk being attacked by coyotes. Next, we heard she was at the hospital. We snuck into the hospital to kill her. Twice!"

"So, all this was Vic's idea? And, you just did what you were told?"

"Yup."

"And you'll testify to all this?"

"Now wait a minute. I'm not sure. I don't want Vic mad at me."

"Oh, he won't be mad. You just tell the truth and it'll be fine," Doug assured him.

Doug and Tom returned to Tom's office to find Finn still seated and waiting for them.

"I thought I told you to go home," Tom said as he stretched his neck from side to side relieving the tension that had grown there.

"I had to know how the questioning went. I won't be able to sleep until I know these guys are going away for good."

"Oh, they will be going away for a long time," Doug guaranteed.

"Well, what's the story?"

Tom and Doug filled him in on what they'd learned from the arrests they'd made that night.

"Our forensics team will no doubt find similar internet links from Sally's iCloud history to other drug involved deaths around the area. They'll be able to find strings of emails that connect them all."

"Wow. They stayed one step ahead of us the whole time we were looking into Jimmy's death," Finn observed.

"We found the receivers for the monitoring devices they used at the house when we made the arrests. As soon as it was reported Jimmy died, and they knew it was from their pills, they got paranoid. They ransacked the community center computers thinking Jimmy had used those. But when they heard Sally tell you that Jimmy used her computer, they got worried the emails and web searches had been found and could be traced back to them.

"Their boss knew what had happened and ordered them to burn the place so the computers would be destroyed. They kidnapped Sally when they realized we were determined to help Sally remember what she found. She was a loose end.

"Forensics is going over every inch of that property next door to you, but they've already reported in that they found traces of the accelerant used in the fire on the bottom of a pair of shoes they found in the basement. They also found similar traces in the van. And, we're certain we'll find Sally's DNA in the van, too. That'll put the nail in the coffin on the arson and kidnapping, not to mention Joe's death. And Nikolai confessed to their plot to go after Sally in the hospital.

"We've got them, Finn. All of them. It was Nora's pictures that gave us the clue we needed to crack the case. She's quite the sketch artist. We'll be sure to thank her ourselves. And, we have DEA agents in Boston right now, picking up this guy Rodney and his partners. We predict their office there is a front for one of the largest drug rings on the East Coast. They were probably looking to expand their territory by moving out here. The partners along with the two clowns we picked up tonight will be charged on dealing drugs. And they're going down for the murders of Jimmy Dalton, Joe, and the young woman in the hospital. They're facing charges for arson and the attempted murders of Sally and Nora, not to mention Sally's kidnapping."

"What about John Casey? What's going to happen to him?" Finn asked, hesitant to know the answer.

"Not sure. He'll be asked to testify. I doubt there will be any charges against him but that's up to the DA."

"What's next?" Finn wondered aloud.

"We all go home and get some rest. You've got a big day tomorrow. Sally and Nora get discharged and you folks have a lot to do to get your lives back in order."

"Oh yeah." Finn agreed unable to hide his grin as he got up to leave. "We've got to rebuild the bakery building, renovate a barn, and get married!"

TWENTY-THREE

The chilly air of December had come roaring in like a lion, building to a blizzard dropping two feet of snow just before the Christmas school break. The high school students filed in first, taking seats in the bleachers that surrounded the gymnasium. Some murmured about having an assembly right before school vacation when they should be having a snow day, while others grumbled about getting another lecture about drugs even if this one wasn't going to be from one of their teachers. Members of the community entered afterwards and sat in the folding chairs that filled the remaining hardwood floor area. Nora and her parents sat front and center with Jen, Mike, and Finn sitting to their side.

Sally stepped up to the microphone, Goldie settling at her feet. Her nerves were calmed by knowing that telling her story might save someone's life. She wanted good to come from all the bad that had occurred. While she didn't want to relive the events of finding Jimmy Dalton's body and what followed, she also thought she might find it healing to share. Knowing that her family and friends were in the audience and that Chief Tom

Bashill and Agent Doug Briggs sat behind her, she had the confidence to proceed.

"Thank you for coming out today for this joint school and community assembly. I'm here to talk to you about drugs. I know you've sat in other assemblies and think you've heard it all before. Today's talk is going to be a little different. I want to talk about fentanyl, a killer that's relentless in getting its grips into our community. Unless we do something to stop it and take action to protect ourselves and our loved ones, it will come for us all, just as it did for one of your classmates.

"Today it's being mixed with every kind of drug you can get on the street or online through drug dealers that look legit on the surface. They're adding it to pills, liquids, powders, gummies, nasal sprays, eye droppers, and candy. It makes drugs cheaper so you'll be more enticed, and they're more addictive so you'll come back for more.

"Let me tell you my story. I was out jogging one day and came across the body of a young man that had his whole life ahead of him. He's someone you all know, a good kid, a hero in the eyes of many. He died of an accidental fentanyl overdose while trying to manage pain from his football injury…"

As Sally wrapped up the telling of her story, Chief Bashill stood and approached the microphone.

"Thank you for sharing your story, Sally," the chief began. "I just have a few words of my own." He cleared his throat before proceeding. "I'd like to take this opportunity to present a Community Service Award to a local hero sitting right here in our midst today. Nora Andersen!"

Everyone clapped. Nora covered her face with her hands and began laughing.

"Nora, you helped the local police and DEA crack this case with your sketches and we just want to say thank you. We have a plaque here with your name that we'll be hanging up at the police station and we have one for you that you can take home along with this stack of new sketch pads and pencils. You really are amazing. Thank you again for all your help with our case."

Everyone clapped. The chief walked the gifts he had for Nora over to her and set them in her lap. Nora squealed with delight. Mr. and Mrs. Andersen reached out to shake the chief's hand in appreciation.

One week later it was Christmas and the day Sally had waited for her entire life had arrived. Dressing in the side room of the church she thought, *How many girls get to marry their lifelong best friend, and on Christmas weekend? To think, it almost didn't happen. What if Finn hadn't come back to the bakery that day?*

Her mother, standing behind her said, "You don't look nervous at all. You're glowing."

"I'm not nervous," Sally told her. "I'm marrying my best friend. I've wanted this my whole life. I am so blessed."

Finally dressed, she took her bouquet of white roses and let her mother lead her to the mirror.

"You are one beautiful bride, my dear," her mother said, dabbing tears from her eyes with her hankie.

Jen and Nora, already dressed, stood in the outer hall in their dark green satin dresses. They looked spectacular in the church with its golden candlelight and red poinsettia plants. Big white bows attached to the pews that lined the aisles.

As guests came in, they seated themselves. Tom arrived with his wife Debra. Meg Bowers joined them followed by Doug, their new friend at the DEA. Mike arrived next and went to where Nora and Jen waited by the side door.

"Hello, ladies. You both look amazing."

"Thanks, Mike," Jen said. Nora's smile was brimming over.

"And Merry Christmas!" he added. "I have a little present for each of you."

"What's this?" Jen asked excitedly.

"Just a little something for you both to say Merry Christmas." He handed them each a small gold foil wrapped box with a gold bow.

Nora and Jen's eyes both grew wide when they saw that Mike had given them each a thin single strand gold bracelet. Jen's bracelet had a petite heart charm hanging from it.

"Wow, Mike," Jen exclaimed, holding up the trinket. "This is lovely, and simple. Just beautiful."

"Here, let me help you put it on." Mike turned first to Nora and attached hers to her wrist and then to Jen to do the same. Jen leaned in to give him a hug. Nora smiled and clapped, her pleasure apparent.

When all the guests were seated, Mike walked Sally's mother down the aisle and then returned to escort Nora and Jen to the front. He couldn't believe how spectacular both women looked, especially Jen. As he took her arm, he felt his heart begin to pound. Once the girls were in their place on the left side at the front of the church, Mike stood to the right with Finn. Goldie, wearing her own green satin bandana, trotted down the aisle, taking a seat on the floor next to Finn, much to the crowd's amusement. Mr. Andersen walked Sally down the aisle in time to Pachelbel's "Canon in D" being played masterfully on cello and piano. Father Joe waited for them, his delight evident on his face.

"Welcome, everyone. We're here today to celebrate the marriage of Sally Andersen and Finn Webster."

A short time later, everyone cheered when the priest finished with, "I now pronounce you husband and wife."

Guests lined up to greet them as they readied to leave the church and head to the newly renovated barn for the reception.

At the last minute, Sally turned and threw her bouquet. It landed right in Jen's arms, causing squeals of laughter and applause from everyone. Finn looked over at Mike and winked. Mike just laughed.

The remodeled barn was the perfect location for the reception. The town council had held off from any further opposition to their plans to develop the event venue on Finn's land.

Now decorated with streams of white flowers and little gold lights, it was everything Finn and Sally had hoped it would be. The kitchen in the back met the needs of the caterer and the alcove for the band provided great acoustic sound.

Amidst the merriment of the wedding, the friends reflected on the past year and wondered what the coming year would bring.

"I thought this day would never get here," Finn said grinning.

"You and me both," Sally added.

"I can't believe what you've been through," Jen mused. "You both deserve this wonderful day."

"We made it because of our faith, family, and friends," Sally reminded them. Smiling she added, "I do wonder about what's next for all of us?"

"How do you feel about horses?" Mike asked.

"Horses?" Finn was puzzled.

"Yup. And maybe some occasional traffic next door?"

"Um…I guess we're okay with that. Why?" Sally asked, her curiosity peaked.

"Well, it looks like you're going to have a new neighbor."

"We are? Who?" Finn was surprised they hadn't heard any word of this before now.

"Me!" Mike laughed, unable to contain his excitement. "I bought the property at auction."

"You're moving here? Wow! That's great," Sally interjected, seeing the huge smile on Jen's face.

"Well, the details aren't all worked out yet, but I'm hoping to open a therapy center," Mike explained. "There's no place around here where people can get help outside of the hospital setting. And there's no more beautiful place than Glen Rock. I think it could help a lot of veterans, or people with disabilities, or those dealing with grief or addiction."

"People connect with animals and the arts," Mike continued. "I'm going to have horses, maybe an art center, or a music studio. I'm not sure. I'm hoping there'll be a linkage with high school kids if they need or want it and we'll connect with other services in the area. There'll be space for counseling sessions and a nice garden. I want to get permits to cut some walking trails into the woods too. It's all in the planning stage, but I've got Nora and Meg helping me put the ideas together. Oh, and the silo's definitely coming down."

The friends laughed and congratulated him. "That all sounds wonderful," Finn said grinning at his friend. "It's good for us, good for you, and good for Glen Rock! So, let's toast!"

"To all of us and the future!" Sally added, lifting her glass to the others.

"Cheers!"

ACKNOWLEDGMENTS

Thank you for reading my book. Starting out as a simple writing prompt, the story came to life almost on its own. Many thanks go out to my husband Rick for his endless support of my writing and for being my sounding board as this story came together. He made writing this story so much fun! Special thanks to my writing friends in the St. Joan of Arc Writer's Group Ministry in Hershey, PA and the Riverwood Writer's Group in Ponte Vedra, Fl who are always encouraging me. And I especially want to thank my friends Bill Leonard, Gary and Marlene Bredfeldt, Jane Robertson, Wayne Parcel, Lisa Perrotti, Ruth Zemba, Neil Ott, Kate Hannisian, Sally Constain, and Fr. Kevin Key for their input, enthusiasm, and encouragement as I made it to the finish line with this project. This story couldn't have come together without all of you and I thank God for blessing me with your love and friendship.

ABOUT THE AUTHOR

The Sketch, A Glen Rock Mystery, was inspired by both Karen's Catholic roots and her time working with people with disabilities, recognizing that we all have valuable gifts to share. Additionally, she was struck by the increasing number of teen deaths related to fentanyl overdoses.

Karen worked as an advocate for people with disabilities and their families for over thirty years. In addition to a BA degree in Social Work, she completed a graduate certificate program in Catholic Theology through the Augustine Institute. She began writing in high school and after winning first prize in a short story contest, creating stories became a hobby in her spare time. She is currently a member of the St Joan of Arc Creative Writer's Group Ministry in Hershey, PA, and the Riverwood Writer's Group in Ponte Vedra, FL. She is also a member of the Catholic Writer's Guild and the Florida Writer's Association.

After retiring from social work, Karen assisted her husband with his landscape and snow plowing company that employed 150 people in Syracuse, NY. During those ten years, she wrote several articles for Snow Business Magazine on topics such as human resource issues and employee safety which she also specialized in. Today she continues to work as a managing partner of Forge Ahead Consulting and Software, assisting others in growing their businesses.

Originally from Salem MA, she currently lives in Ponte Vedra, Fl with her husband. They have four sons and several grandchildren who all live in various parts of the country. Her other hobbies include hiking in the mountains and walking the coastal beaches. She also enjoys RV travel with her husband throughout the country. When not traveling, she volunteers for local community organizations.

Milton Keynes UK
Ingram Content Group UK Ltd.
UKHW030636071024
449371UK00001B/7